"Merry Lattimore, I hereby bind you over for trial before the Sessions Court. You are to be committed to Newgate gaol until such time as your case is heard."

The single crack of his gavel sounded as final as a blow from the executioner's ax.

With a grimly satisfied smile, Mrs. Paget flounced from his courtroom, followed closely by her son.

Merry remained motionless. The horror on her face cut Graham to the quick. "Your imprisonment won't last long. The Sessions are to be held in but three days."

Her eyes narrowed and she leaned forward, brow furrowed. A constable took her arm and escorted her from the dock. She accompanied him without protest, but shot one more look over her shoulder as she was pulled away. Their gazes met for an instant, and Graham knew she had finally recognized him.

LISA KARON RICHARDSON

is an award-winning author and a member of American Christian Fiction Writers. Influenced by books like *The Little Princess,* Lisa's early books were heavy on creepy boarding schools. Though she's mostly all grown-up now, she still loves a healthy dash of adventure in any story she creates, even her real-life story. She's been a missionary to the Seychelles and Gabon and now that she and her husband are back in America, they are tackling new adventures—starting a daughter-work church and raising two precocious kids. Visit her online at www.lisakaronrichardson.com.

The Magistrate's Folly

Lisa Karon Richardson

Heartsong Presents

For my family, who are so accommodating of my dreams. To my Mom and Dad who have never ceased to believe in me. You gave me the confidence to try. For my Grandpa Shoemaker and Grandma Dixie, no one could have better cheerleaders. I'm lucky to have you in my life. And finally to the "Inkies," I love you all. Thanks to every one of you for your support and encouragement.

A note from the Author:

I love to hear from my readers! You may correspond with me by writing:

Lisa Karon Richardson
Author Relations
P.O. Box 9048
Buffalo, NY 14240-9048

ISBN-13: 978-0-373-48647-2

THE MAGISTRATE'S FOLLY

This edition issued by special arrangement with Barbour Publishing, Inc., 1810 Barbour Drive, Uhrichsville, Ohio, U.S.A.

All scripture quotations are taken from the King James Version of the Bible.

PRINTED IN THE U.S.A.

Prologue

February 6, 1773
London, England

From his perch above the fray, Graham Sinclair eyed his courtroom. The shabbiness of his domain mocked his dreams of justice. The cracksman he had just bound over for trial was two-thirds drunk and staggering. It wasn't justice. It was farce.

"Next case." He kneaded the bridge of his nose and shut his eyes. The usual shuffles and thumps were accompanied by the usual muted uproar from the waiting mob. These few moments between cases always reminded him of a scene change at the theater. Would comedy or tragedy play out next?

He sighed. He had his role to perform just as the other players in the drama.

He opened his eyes and sought Connor. His old friend and

assistant nodded, and Graham cleared his throat. Connor slid a document before him.

"Mrs. Paget." Graham glanced from the brief in his hands to the accuser, a woman in middle years who wore a pinched expression as if her stays were too tight. As he regarded her, she sniffed and raised a handkerchief to her nose with excessive delicateness. The venomous glance she cast at the noisy throng of victims and vagabonds, constables and criminals milling on the other side of the railing might have wilted the lot—had they noticed.

Graham lifted his gaze to the raised dock directly before him. He blinked and looked again. A slight figure stood there, head held high. Surely he knew that auburn hair and those fiercely determined brown eyes.

His finger ran down the document as he sought the name of the accused. "Merry Lattimore." He whispered the name aloud as he read it. He dropped the paper, making no move to catch it as it fluttered to the ground.

He sought her face once more, searching for something, anything, that would put the lie to her claim of identity. She seemed not to recognize him. But then it had been years since they had last seen each other.

Connor placed the retrieved document before him and gave him an odd look.

Graham cleared his throat. "Are the accusers present?"

"We are, Your Honor." The plaintiffs' singsong chant sounded like a chorus of smug Eton lads.

"Of what does the prisoner stand accused?"

"Theft from her mistress," Connor said in his official voice.

Graham looked again at the prosecution bench. "You are Mrs. Paget?"

"Yes, Excellency."

"*Your Honor* will do."

The woman came perilously close to shrugging.

"You stand as accuser of this young woman?" His severest frown, which had quailed hardened cutthroats, had no marked effect on her.

"Yes, Your Honor."

"State your case."

The woman's chin jutted out farther. "This morning I discharged Merry Lattimore from my employ. I gave her time to pack her belongings. I then retired to the drawing room to recover my nerves from the unpleasant scene she made." She paused a moment as if to gauge his reaction.

"A few moments later, my son came to me and stated that he had seen her sneaking from my room. I assure you she had no cause to be in my chambers. I went in search of her and apprehended the little baggage as she was about to leave the house. She claimed her valise contained only her things. Indeed, she acted as if I were in the wrong." Outrage turned her voice brittle.

She sniffed and raised a handkerchief to her nose. "As soon as my son opened it, I found several pieces of my jewelry right there on top."

"Is that all you have to say?"

She looked confused, as if wondering what other proof he could possibly desire. "Yes."

"Have you any other witnesses to call?"

"My son, Lucas."

Lucas Paget took his mother's place.

Graham could not quite name why the man should be so off-putting. He looked like any of a thousand other louts with more money than sense. His pea-green jacket was embroidered with wildflowers; his pale satin breeches shone. His lace cuffs dripped over his hands, as languid as their wearer.

He recounted his tale of seeing Merry sneaking from his mother's room.

"Why was Miss Lattimore discharged from employment?"

Scarlet suffused the young man's face. "Immoral conduct."

Graham narrowed his eyes. Not the Merry he'd known. She had her faults. He knew that more than most, but she would not easily thrust aside her virtue. "And those scratches on your cheek? Where did they come from?"

"I don't see that it has any bearing on the theft." Paget took a pinch of snuff from an enameled box and sniffed.

"I can see why you might think so." Graham fought to keep the contempt from his tone. He'd have laid money that Merry had discouraged an unwanted advance. That was the real cause of her dismissal. But then why the accusation of theft? It made no sense. Unless she had taken the items in misguided retribution for getting the boot.

Paget's lips compressed into an ugly sneer.

"Have you anything else to add?" Graham said.

"No."

The constable who had taken Merry in charge was called, and he attested to being summoned to the house and seeing the jewelry in Miss Lattimore's bag.

Graham groaned inwardly. The Pagets' case was strong. What possible explanation could Merry produce to excuse herself? He had to find some way to help her. He owed her father that much.

In the curve of her lips and arch of her brow he again saw the carefree girl he had known. How had she been reduced to such circumstances?

Two spots of crimson burned brightly in her otherwise pale cheeks, and he could see the white of her knuckles as they clutched the railing. She stood unmoving in the dock. Was it possible that she had not moved since the proceedings started?

"Have you anything to say in your defense, Miss Lattimore?" He smiled. Nodded. *Come along, girl. Exonerate yourself.*

She met his gaze without flinching. Still he saw no hint of recognition in her eyes. Had he changed so much? Mayhap it was his stiff, white judicial wig. It tended to obscure the man beneath his office.

"I took nothing from the Pagets. Indeed, I was leaving without even the wages I had earned."

"And would you happen to know how Mr. Paget received the injuries to his face?"

The carmine blotches in her cheeks bled into the rest of her face. "Yes." The answer was little more than a whisper.

He had expected as much. "Please explain."

Merry closed her eyes and inhaled deeply, as if she needed the fortification of extra breath in her lungs. When she opened her eyes again, the color in her cheeks had drained, leaving her skin ivory pale.

"I caused the injuries in the course of discouraging his advances."

An outraged murmur issued from the plaintiff's bench, and Graham held up his hand for silence.

"How do you explain the presence of the jewelry in your case?"

"I cannot explain it. I don't know how it came to be there."

"Did you pack the bag yourself?" Silently he willed her to give him something to work with.

"I did."

A muscle in his jaw ticked. "And was it in your possession until you attempted to leave the house?"

"No."

Ah, finally the first ray of hope. "Please explain."

"I placed my bag on the table in the foyer as I went to say farewell to some fri—" Merry's gaze flickered toward Mrs. Paget. "Fellow servants in the kitchen before I departed."

"How long was your bag unattended?"

"A few moments."

"Were there other people about?"

"Yes, Your Honor."

"Is it possible that someone else placed the jewelry in your bag?"

"It's possible. Indeed, it is the only explanation, but I don't know who would do such a thing. At least…" Her voice sank, and she seemed to be talking half to herself. "Surely it was enough to see me out the door?"

Graham quieted the impulse to rub his temples. Was she intent on a visit to Tyburn's gallows?

"Did you see anyone near your valise when you came to retrieve it?"

"No sir."

Graham sighed deeply. There was no help for it now. He had tried to aid her, but he had no choice. There wasn't a scrap of evidence to support her.

His throat seemed suddenly as parched and dusty as a volume on legal ethics. "Merry Lattimore, I hereby bind you over for trial before the Sessions Court. You are to be committed to Newgate gaol until such time as your case is heard." The single crack of his gavel sounded as final as a blow from the executioner's ax.

With a grimly satisfied smile, Mrs. Paget flounced from his courtroom, followed closely by her son.

Merry remained motionless. The horror on her face cut Graham to the quick. "Your imprisonment won't last long. The Sessions are to be held in but three days."

Her eyes narrowed and she leaned forward, brow furrowed. A constable took her arm and escorted her from the dock. She accompanied him without protest, but shot one more look over her shoulder as she was pulled away. Their gazes met for an instant, and Graham knew she had finally recognized him.

Chapter 1

May 12, 1773
Yorktown, Virginia Colony

Had Merry arrived in Virginia under different circumstances she might have been charmed. The bustling port told of prosperity. Sailors and porters jostled one another with cargoes of Caribbean sugar, British silver, and East Indian teas. The sun graced the town with a loving favor it never seemed to shower on London.

Despite the predawn hour, the breeze held only a hint of coolness and coaxed her cloak from her shoulders for the first time in months. Flowers blossomed in all directions, declaring spring and new hope.

The irony wasn't lost upon her.

She took a half-dozen steps toward a tree with enormous, glossy, dark leaves and large, sweetly scented white flowers. Her physician father had instilled in her a love of all things botanical, along with an understanding of their medicinal properties. What healing powers might these new species contain?

A sailor's calloused hand snatched her up short. "Where do you think you're going? You've an appointment in Williamsburg." He laughed.

She was shackled in line with seventy-three other prisoners and herded through Yorktown and into the countryside. The forced march made her legs and lungs burn. She hadn't had so much exercise in ages. Yet, even the indignity of the manacles could not quite dim her curiosity. Magnificent oaks draped with some sort of feathery, ethereal plant stood like guardians on either side of the road. Was that some sort of moss? Her fingers itched to search one of Father's old books for the plant's name.

The man in front of her staggered, jerking her attention to him. She steadied him with a hand to his elbow while trying not to trip over his floundering limbs. The prisoner behind her thumped into her back.

For the first time since their landing, Merry took notice of her fellow captives. Scant food and the fetid air belowdecks had enfeebled them. Most shambled forward, heads down, faces distorted with filth and despair. She glanced back at the man who had bumped her. His eyes were so glazed he seemed barely aware of his own movement, much less his surroundings.

She had only been saved from the same fate through the friendship of Sarah Proctor. They had grown close in Newgate when Merry nursed Sarah through a bout of malignant quinsy. She missed Sarah's practical company now. But her friend, though a convict, had had money set by. Sarah had paid for them both to share a small cabin and receive edible food. And now she had paid her own ransom, and would not have to suffer the indignity of an indenture. She had offered to pay Merry's ransom as well, but Merry could not bring herself to saddle Sarah with her upkeep, too. Now Merry questioned that decision.

At last a cluster of whitewashed houses, gleaming in the sun, heralded the beginning of a neat little town. Far from the crudeness Merry had expected, the town was built in fashionable style. Large clapboard homes with numerous windows watched over tidy streets. The town felt crisp and new, completely unlike London's jaded urbanity.

Passersby eyed the long file of prisoners, but without the derision they had endured in London. Here they were worthy of neither scorn nor compassion—no more or less than livestock for sale.

They were driven to a market green at the heart of the town. Most of the prisoners collapsed to the ground. They sounded miserable as they gasped for air. The guards had given them no water all morning.

Merry found the six other women from the ship, and they huddled together.

A stream of well-heeled customers flowed around them like water surrounding an island. Despite the warmth of the day, Merry nearly took refuge beneath her cloak. But the guards would only have taken it from her. It was plain they wanted the wares on display, though the scrutiny of the strolling men stripped her to the core.

How had she been reduced to this?

Why?

Her tongue swelled in her mouth and her cheeks burned. Torn between the desire to disappear and the desire to shout her accomplishments, so as to obtain a good place, she trembled and sat still.

For the first time in months she muttered a prayer. A last resort. But she could summon no conviction. And the supplication dribbled away as Merry's grief lodged in her throat.

The heat wilted all but the strongest of the convicts. Dust

stirred up by dray horses and carts and a thousand feet rose into the air, clogging her nose and mouth. Merry fanned herself with her free hand, but there was no relief to be had.

An elderly man some ten feet from Merry was the first to faint. Two others soon followed.

A wealthy tradesman wearing a violently purple waistcoat poked the man with his cane. "Weak stock."

His companion nodded as if soaking in words of wisdom.

Merry shot to her feet, irons jangling. Sarah had taught her how to handle importunate men. " 'Ere now, cully, you leave us be, or I'll scratch yer eyes out." She glared at the man with all the impotent fury she had nursed in the last three months.

The man's eyes widened. "How dare you."

"Get." Lips pulled back in a snarl, Merry jerked her head toward the street.

"Hoyden! You'll regret this display." The man led his friend away to the captain. His gesticulations and furtive glances made it clear he was reporting her behavior.

Merry continued to stand, head held high, though her heart pounded in her throat.

The captain stalked toward her. "What's all this then?"

"Sir, that gentleman was most offensive." Without giving him time to offer a rebuke she continued. "Pray tell, do you wish to make a profit on this human cargo?"

The question and her genteel accent seemed to confuse the man.

Merry went on, "I ask because you have done yourself a disservice. These people will be more lively and active if they are given some water. And that can only translate into more money for your coffers. If you wish, I would be willing to draw and distribute the water."

He eyed her for a long moment as if trying to comprehend what fraud she was plotting. At last he gave a short jerk of his head. "Very well. But a guard will go with you."

Merry nodded. It was no more than she had expected.

With the guard at her side, Merry took her place in the line for the pump. She filled a bucket to the brim and drank deeply. Even warm, the water felt glorious as it swept away the grit. Arms wrapped around the bucket, she hefted it up. She staggered and water sloshed over her, drenching her bodice.

Trying not to spill any more of the precious liquid, she hauled it back to the cluster of prisoners. They drank gratefully, greedily—slurping at the water and sighing as if they had never tasted anything so sweet. They soaked their kerchiefs in it and wiped their faces, eyes closing in delight.

Merry moved to the next person in the row and then the next. She refilled the bucket twice more and succeeded in giving them all a drink before her guardian insisted she return to her place. She put her hands to her aching back. Kneeling and bending with the bucket had become tedious long ago.

No sooner had she settled among her fellows again than the auction began. One by one the prisoners were led to the block. Merry turned away, stomach churning.

Inevitably, her turn came. She hesitated in climbing onto the block, and the guard prodded her forward. Her hands were damp, her throat dry again.

Men and women milled about the square, some looking prosperous, others mercenary. Most seemed to be in search of a specific type of servant. They gossiped and debated with friends until the convict they wished to bid for was put up.

The auctioneer's voice boomed preternaturally loud by her ear. "Name: Merry Lattimore, transported after conviction for larceny. Term of indenture is to be seven years. Former employment: governess. Can read and write and do sums. Some knowledge of herbs and physic. Age: twenty-two years. She is in good health. Unmarried. No children."

Merry cringed to be reduced to such a paltry accounting.

"Bidding will start at ten pounds."

Less than a good dray horse.

"Ten pounds."

Merry ripped her gaze from the ground. She knew that voice. It was the tradesman in the purple waistcoat, and he had a nasty gleam in his eye.

Connor made a sharp gesture, catching Graham's eye. After seeing the lad before him led away in manacles, Graham rose and rubbed his eyes. For an instant, as the door opened and the boy stepped outside, all Graham could see was Merry Lattimore's slight form as she had passed through those same doors. The two months since her ship had sailed for America had helped not a whit. The memory of her wounded gaze haunted him.

Retreating to his office, he placed his wig on its pedestal. The door behind him opened, and he turned to see Connor. His friendship with the former thief had begun when Graham had taken his part in a brawl with one of the local bully boys, but had deepened immeasurably since Connor had attended a Methodist meeting, given up theft, and come to work for Graham.

"What is it?" Graham hung his judicial robe on its hook.

"You remember them Pagets what had some jewelry stolen a couple months back."

Graham stiffened and turned to face his friend. "Yes."

"It's gone missin' again."

Graham gaped as if the report had been spouted in Dutch. "What?"

Connor smirked, a disquieting expression on his pugnacious features. "Thought that girl got to you. You've been sulking ever since you heard her case. Not your usual pleasant self, one might say."

Graham wished heartily that he could protest, but it was true. "I knew her father...."

"So you said." Connor shrugged and turned to the door. "I can send one of the lads to look into the matter."

Drat the man. "No. I'll investigate." Graham snatched his waistcoat and shoved in his arms.

A wicked grin curved Connor's mouth until it resembled a devil's horns. "I thought as much. I told the constable we'd be over straightaway."

It didn't take long to find the pawnbroker who had bought the jewels and determine that Lucas Paget had been behind the theft. Graham had the weasel brought to the office for questioning.

Tears poured from the fellow as if someone had primed a pump. "I fell into a game of high stakes with a group of, well, they were no gentlemen." He sniffled into his handkerchief.

"Get on with it."

"The blackguards would not take my offer of payment with my next allowance. They wanted the blunt and threatened…extreme measures if I did not procure it right away."

Graham narrowed his eyes. "Beau traps will usually give more grace."

Paget refused to meet his gaze, and a dull red blanketed his features. "They somehow got the idea I was trying to gull them by sleight of hand."

"So they caught you cheating and ordered you to pay up or else."

Paget nodded miserably.

"Why didn't you simply ask your mother for the wherewithal?"

"And listen to her bleating on about it until the end of time?"

"So you determined to stage a burglary."

"I was going to buy it all back next month when my quarterly allowance comes in. It would have been no loss to her."

Something Paget had said swirled to the forefront of Graham's thoughts. "It was you!" He grasped his hands behind his back to keep himself from throttling the rogue.

"I...yes, I admit I took the jewelry."

"No, I mean you were the one who put the jewelry in Merry Lattimore's bag. With your sleight of hand tricks you slipped the things inside as you opened it."

Paget licked his lips.

Graham's hands balled into fists. "She could have been sent to the gallows. And all because she did not allow you to defile her?"

"It wasn't that," Lucas wailed. "She found out I had been gaming. She'd have told mother of my...problems at the table. I had to discredit her."

The image of Merry answering the accusations put to her, head high and eyes snapping with wounded dignity, rose before Graham then faded into a red haze.

"C'mon. Graham, let 'im go."

Graham blinked, and Connor's face sprang into his line of sight.

"Let 'im go. He'll get his in Newgate."

Graham released Paget, and the wretch fell back into his chair, choking and whimpering.

"Take him away, Connor." Graham collapsed into one of the other chairs before the fireplace. "I cannot hear his case. Take him to Bow Street."

Connor led a defeated Paget away, one hand on his collar.

Graham stared into the fire. He had taken part in condemning Merry Lattimore unjustly. The guilt of it nearly bent him in two. He slid to his knees. Dear Lord, she was a thousand miles from home, at the mercy of heaven only knew what kind of master. What had he done? He put his head in his hands. "God, help me to make it right."

Chapter 2

Merry breathed in through her nose. No. No. No. Her gaze met the tradesman's. One side of his nose ticked up in a sneer.

"I have ten pounds from Mr. Cleaves."

She hunched in on herself as if someone had punched her in the stomach. She was going to be hauled away by the vindictive little man and worked to death in tobacco fields.

Or worse.

A fly buzzed around her, and she focused on it. The tiny creature was incredibly ugly—no doubt he would be swatted by one of the men present, and still his future seemed brighter than her own.

"Eleven pounds."

The cool, female voice slid over Merry, as refreshing as her first drink of water by the pump. She raised her head, eyes searching for the speaker. Against her will a flicker of hope ignited.

"Twelve." A querulous note raised Cleaves's voice.

"Thirteen."

This time Merry found the speaker. A petite, elegantly clad woman near the rear of the crowd. A tall slave woman stood at the lady's side holding a parasol over her perfectly coifed hair.

"Fifteen." Blotches of red stained Cleaves's cheekbones.

"Eighteen."

"Twenty."

"Twenty-five."

The crowd murmured.

Cleaves's nostrils flared. His lips twitched, but he said nothing.

"Twenty-five pounds, once… Twice… To Mrs. Benning for twenty-five pounds."

The auctioneer nudged Merry and jerked his thumb toward the left. Knees trembling so that she nearly toppled from the platform, she shuffled toward a clerk who sat behind a small table, filling out the legal documents of indenture and accepting payment. The swish of skirts made her turn.

Her new mistress approached, her gaze focused not on Merry but on the man at the table. Mrs. Benning discussed payment arrangements for a long moment before suddenly turning and prodding the manacles that bound Merry's wrists. "I don't think we will need these, do you, Merry?"

Merry licked her lips. "No madam."

The shackles were removed and clunked down among the documents, nearly upsetting the clerk's inkpot.

Merry chaffed her wrists. She kept her eyes downcast, unsure of the etiquette of such a situation. "I am grateful for your kindness."

Mrs. Benning made no sign she had heard. Half-bent over the table, she wielded the quill with a flourish, signing the document presented to her. With a curt nod toward Merry and her slave woman she marched away from the market green, leaving them to scurry after her.

A landau awaited Mrs. Benning just outside a tidy brick church. A young black man in handsome livery perched in the coachman's seat. He scrambled down at their approach and swung the door open for Mrs. Benning. She climbed in without a word, and the lad closed the door behind her.

Uncertain what to do, Merry halted in midstep. Was she expected to walk? The Negress met her gaze for the first time and indicated with a jerk of her chin that they were to sit on the board at the back, where in London a footman might have stood.

"Home, Crawford."

"Yes'm." The coachman hopped back up to his place and whipped the horses into a canter.

The carriage lurched forward, and Merry snatched at the side before she slid right off her precarious seat. Her paltry bundle of belongings skidded toward the edge, and the Negress snatched it back. She seemed unaffected by the movement.

The meager contents of Merry's stomach sloshed about, making her regret the water she had drunk. She swallowed, and swallowed again. She could not disgrace herself. Her knuckle showed bone white as her hands gripped the seat.

In truth, she couldn't say if it was the motion of the cart or apprehension that unsettled her. What lay in store for her next? Was the ordeal drawing to a close or merely beginning?

Swaying slightly, Merry clambered from her seat to face an enormous white house on a broad, well-kempt street. No neighbors squashed up next to it as they were prone to do in London. Instead, she could see the edge of a garden and several outbuildings behind the main structure. Black shutters framed wide, arched windows. Gray shingles ran up the mansard roof, parting to allow four dormer windows to peek out over the street.

Merry stared at the imposing facade. She felt as if all her emotions had been forced through a strainer, leaving only a leaden, remote sort of apathy.

Mrs. Benning turned at the top step and glanced around. She caught Merry's gaze and made an impatient come-here motion with two fingers. As if the imperious gesture had broken some sort of spell, Merry found her legs capable of movement and followed her new mistress inside.

Mrs. Benning led the way into an elegant room painted a cheerful green. She settled onto a divan. "I imagine you would like to know a bit about your new situation."

"Yes madam. If you please." Merry stood in the center of the room, hands knit loosely in front of her.

"I believe you would do well as a nanny. My Emma is five and John, three. They are bright, precocious children, but they require firm guidance."

"Yes madam."

"You will teach them to read and write and some basic arithmetic. I will expect them to be clean and well-fed, their days to be regulated. But don't forget that they are children."

Merry nodded, not trusting herself to open her mouth. So many questions were piled in her head that if she spoke one would surely tumble out.

"The Benning name is respected throughout the colonies. We have high standards. I had not intended to indenture a convict when I went to market today."

"Why did you?" The words were out before Merry could blink. She would have given her last shilling to recall them.

Mrs. Benning's cool blue eyes surveyed Merry, and the slightest smile quirked one corner of her mouth before disappearing. "I saw you."

Merry frowned. What was she to make of that?

"I saw you tending the other convicts."

A blush heated Merry's face. "I...the heat." She failed to keep the defensiveness from her tone. "They needed water or—"

"I am not critical. Your kindness recalled to mind the story of Rebekah watering all those camels. I felt all at once as if I must purchase your indenture. That, and I detest Thomas Cleaves—dreadful man."

A jumble of new questions rendered Merry speechless.

"That being said, I must make some inquiries. The charge of which you were convicted was larceny?"

"Yes." Merry looked away. She would ever be bound by the accusation, whether physical chains chaffed her wrists or not.

"Please tell me about it."

Merry did, as concisely as possible. Mrs. Benning's mouth quirked again, but not with a smile, when she heard Merry's protests of innocence. No doubt every convict in Virginia heralded their innocence. At least her new mistress had the consideration not to laugh.

When Merry came to the end of her recital, Mrs. Benning regarded her for a long moment. Could she see anything beyond the filth of the convict hulk?

Was there anything else anymore?

"My woman, Jerusha, will show you what is expected."

The slave woman led the way from the sitting room. Acutely aware of her grubbiness, Merry licked her lips and smoothed her skirts. Nervous fingers tried to push the stray locks of hair back from her face, but without a glass it was difficult to say whether she was making matters better or worse.

On the third floor the slave woman swung open a door. "Here's the nursery. You'll sleep in here with the children." She indicated a thin pallet in the corner.

Jaunty yellow walls were broken by a series of tall windows that allowed light to stream in. Two narrow beds were covered with white coverlets and fluffy bolsters. A spindly chair sat between the beds. In the middle of the room a tiny table complete with miniature tea service sat atop a pretty floral carpet. A dollhouse sat in one corner near a rocking horse. Toy soldiers were scattered about, apparently where they had fallen in battle.

"This is very nice," Merry said.

"I'll see about finding you something to wear." Jerusha patted Merry's arm.

The human contact was almost more than Merry could bear. Tears welled in her eyes. "Thank you."

She took a seat in the rickety chair, which held up better than she had feared. Absently she stroked the soft coverlet. Mayhap the staff would disapprove of the notion of placing impressionable children in the charge of a convicted felon.

In her heart, she scarcely blamed them. Who could be expected to embrace a thief?

With Jerusha's help, Merry found new clothing and water for a bath.

Delight of delights.

Merry scrubbed with lye soap until her skin was raw and her fingers shriveled. It took an age, but at last she felt as if she had rid herself of the gaol's stink. Between the bath and Jerusha's kindness she felt nearly human again.

She turned as a slight slave girl shepherded the Benning children into the nursery, though she was little older than they.

The children had the same brown hair and gray eyes as their mother, but vivacity gave them a unique comeliness.

Gentle hands turned the children to face Merry. "Emma, John, this is Merry. She's gonna take care of you."

"I don't want her, Hattie. I want you." Little John whirled back to the girl with outstretched hands.

* * *

Graham stood on the deck of the *King's Favor*, staring back at Portsmouth's harbor. His fingers clutched the ship's rail as Merry's had clutched the railing of the dock.

Was he utterly daft? He had asked the question of himself at least twice a day since deciding on this rash course of action. Even as he had made the many preparations required before abandoning his magistracy to a temporary replacement.

Despite the most diligent search, he had been unable to determine much of Merry's fate. The intelligence had left him little choice; the hunt could not be picked up on this side of the Atlantic. But rather than search for a reliable agent to continue the quest in Virginia, Graham had known with a certainty that defied explanation that he must finalize the matter. He would never rest until his error had been made right.

His mind drifted to the last time he had planned a meeting with Merry. Yes, that last visit to the Lattimore house still rankled.

Mrs. Lattimore had skewered him with a glare as sharp as a surgeon's scalpel even as her lips bent in an unwilling smile. "I'm sure you understand, Mr. Sinclair. I have my heart set on this match. As a true friend of this family I know you will also want the best for Merry."

In the pocket of his waistcoat the ring he had purchased so hopefully seemed to singe his flesh right through the cloth. It gave rise to a painful flush that scalded his cheeks as if he were a schoolboy guilty of some monstrous prank.

She continued. "Lord Carroll and his father, the earl, have been more than willing to talk terms. Merry and Dr. Lattimore are down at the Dabney estate in Kent even now, and as you know, her father has determined to settle a very handsome dowry on her when she marries."

Her fan stirred the air, and dust motes scattered to escape the vortex she created. Graham focused on those tiny points of light, trying to maintain his sanity as she prattled.

"I thought you ought to know what was happening. I've noticed how she has led you on. But really the two of you would never have made much of a match. You can see that, I'm sure. She's set her cap for Lord Carroll, and in time you'll be as happy for her as I am." Her voice had turned as pointed as her gaze. "I'm sure you will do nothing to mar her chances. This will mean everything for her." She broadened her smile. "Won't you stay for tea?"

He croaked some reply and all but stumbled from the house in his haste to be away.

He blinked. Even now it pained him that Merry's mother had fended off his advances, as if he weren't a friend but some overeager fellow who needed to be beaten off with a stick.

"You're not brooding again."

"Not at all." Graham rounded on his companion. Trust Connor to hit the nail on the head. Particularly if it was aimed at something sensitive.

Connor placed a heavy hand on his shoulder. "You're doing the right thing."

Graham breathed deep, sucking in the freshening breeze. "My thanks, friend." He smiled. "There is still opportunity for you to turn back if you wish."

"Not I. Who would keep you on the straight and narrow if I'm not there?"

"You make an excellent point." Graham slapped him on the back.

As the last bit of land disappeared from the horizon, Graham led the way belowdecks. What would Merry say when she saw him again?

Chapter 3

September 2, 1773
Williamsburg, Virginia Colony

Merry sat on the edge of the bed, holding a porcelain bowl near John's small, flushed face. Abigail Benning bent over her son, her face a study in worry as she administered a dose of ipecacuanha.

The emetic worked quickly, and Merry handed Abigail a clean linen towel, which she used to wipe his mouth. His languor clenched at her heart even more than the flush that bruised his cheeks an ugly purple-red. Everything had been done. He'd been bled; wrapped in cool, damp flannels; sweated; and purged, yet nothing seemed to loosen the fever's hold. That morning they had undertaken the journey from the Bennings' plantation, where they spent summers, back to town in the hopes that a change of air would effect an improvement.

Another fit of the miserable, whooping cough pushed him forward beneath its weight. Merry glanced up and met Abigail's gaze. "We must resort to the laudanum."

Mrs. Benning raised a hand to rub her forehead, but she nodded.

Merry hurried to the large closet that had been set aside as a stillroom. She had brewed the laudanum in anticipation, though she had hoped not to need it. Her hand shook as she took up the dark brown bottle.

In the nursery, Abigail took the bottle in hands that trembled even more than Merry's. She dosed her son then collapsed in the chair between the beds, looking from one child to the other and back again. Her lips moved soundlessly in prayer, as if her fear was so deep she could not bring herself to utter it aloud.

Emma's dinner tray was brought in, and Abigail waved Merry away, busying herself with helping her daughter eat. Perhaps it was just as well Merry had never been graced with her own family. The naked ache in Abigail's eyes was too raw to endure. Merry didn't know if she could have survived such grief.

Merry opened the jar of garlic salve and rubbed a generous amount onto John's wrists and feet, wrapping them in strips of cotton so the virtue would not be lost. The laudanum had already proved effective. He slept through her ministrations. His breathing was easier, and he seemed in a deep sleep. The coughing was noticeably absent. A good thing. His little body needed rest.

Emma fell asleep after eating a portion of gruel. Her mother knelt by the bed and stroked the girl's soft cheek. As if the weight of her own head had grown too heavy, Abigail leaned her elbows against the counterpane and dropped her head down against her balled fists.

"I can't do it." She turned her haggard face toward Merry.

"Ma'am?"

"I cannot lose another child." The harshness of her tone lanced the sickbed silence of the room like wind sweeping away a fog.

Merry knelt beside Abigail, wishing, longing to be able to comfort her in some way, but she could not find the words. Could not offer hope when she held so little herself. She smoothed the stray hair away from Abigail's face, much as the woman had so recently done for her daughter.

"We will do all we can and leave the rest to God." A hard fate as far as Merry was concerned, but Abigail needed to hear something.

October 6, 1773
Williamsburg, Virginia Colony

Merry rubbed her forehead with the heel of her hand. The danger had passed, but her body ached as if she had been in a bare-knuckle ring with the disease and taken a beating.

Emma held out her slice of bread. "I want jam."

"I don't think so, sweet. It wouldn't sit well, and you don't want to be sick again."

Emma pursed her lips, obviously weighing the matter. Her thin little shoulders heaved in a sigh. "When?"

Merry tapped her bottom lip. "Perhaps tomorrow if you are strong enough."

"Promise?"

"I promise to try to make sure you're well enough."

"I want jam, too." John's lower lip pushed forward, and Merry welcomed the sight. He hadn't had the strength to be pugnacious in days, poor lamb.

She reached out to stroke his hair. "I shall make the same terms I made with your sister. No more, no less."

His lips pursed for a moment; then he nodded. "Tell us a story."

"Which one would you like to hear?"

" 'The Lion and the Mouse.' "

"Very well then." Merry resettled in her chair and smoothed her skirts.

From out in the hall came a rustle and a thump. Merry turned her head toward the noise. Someone must have stumbled and dropped something.

John tugged on her sleeve.

"Once upon a time there was a mighty lion—the king of the jungle. One day he was out hunting when he captured a tiny little mouse."

A strangled sob and hissing whispers pricked Merry's ears. She put up a hand. "Just a moment."

She padded on silent feet to the door and eased it open. Jerusha's son, Daniel, stood in the hall, head bent close to Hattie's. Misery weighed down his features, making him look a wizened old man, rather than a thirteen-year-old boy.

"What's all this?"

They whirled to her, faces etched with terror. Merry glanced down the hallway in both directions. "Come in here, both of you."

Hattie's shoulders still shook, but she and Daniel did as bidden.

"Now, tell me what's wrong."

"Mas…Master Benning." Hattie hiccuped. "He's selling Daniel."

Merry covered her mouth with her hand. "When did you hear this?"

Hattie bent over, hand covering her mouth to stifle her sobs.

Daniel took up the story. "Master and Missus were in the garden, and Mama sent Hattie to take Mrs. Benning a shawl.

She overheard them arguin' 'bout it." Merry could well identify with the pain that brimmed in his eyes.

How would Jerusha bear it? This boy was her life's blood. If he was sent off somewhere, they might never see each other again. It would kill her.

"Does your mama know?"

He nodded, and then his chin began to tremble and he dissolved into tears. John and Emma came in behind her and clutched at her skirts, staring at the older children. Merry had thought her tears were spent, but apparently this was one thing the Lord meant to pour into her with abundance.

John and Emma began to cry then, too, though they did not know the reason. Gathering all four children to her along with the shreds of her emotions, Merry murmured meaningless soothing noises, until the worst of the storm passed.

The old questions that had plagued her sprang back to mind, poking and prodding. How could God allow such a thing to happen?

As the children subsided into hiccuping and sniffling, she settled them all around the nursery table with milk and biscuits. If Mr. Benning found the slaves eating and drinking in common with his own children, she would likely be sent to the tobacco fields, but it mattered not. They were all children in need of comfort.

"Daniel, where is your mother?"

The boy shrugged. "Slaves' hall maybe."

"Children, I'll be back in a bit. Be good and obey Hattie."

Merry found Jerusha in the slaves' hall, sitting stock-still in an old, oft-mended rocking chair. Her gaze was trained out the window, past the gardens and woods, out to the tobacco fields that stretched to the horizon. She was not weeping, but her eyes were red-rimmed, and she held a sopping wet handkerchief in a clawlike grip.

A bevy of slave women outside the hall tried to prevent

Merry's intrusion, but she insisted that she must see her friend. In the five months since she had arrived in Virginia, it had been Jerusha who had kept her sane. The woman had sheltered and taught and helped Merry as she found her footing in this new land and station in life. Jerusha had made the staff accept her by sheer force of will. Without her, Merry was certain she'd have succumbed to despair.

"Jerusha." The single word seemed to get lost in the gulf of grief that surrounded the slave woman, even though she was only a few feet away.

Merry ventured another step into the room. "Daniel told me what's happened. What do you want to do about this?"

The question turned her head. "Do? What can I do? My boy…" Jerusha bent over her knees. The bones and tendons of her fingers stood out in stark relief as she dug into the material of her skirt.

Merry approached and knelt by the rocking chair, encircling Jerusha with one arm and offering her free hand. Jerusha clutched it, hanging on as if it were the whipping post. Faced with another mother about to lose her child, Merry once more found herself unable to speak. She could only be there to hear the words when, and if, they came.

When the torrent of sobs finally quieted, Jerusha released her hand and buried her eyes within her handkerchief. Hand hidden in a fold of her skirt, Merry flexed her fingers. They would be bruised later.

"I never thought this would happen. Not to me and my boy." Shredded by mourning, Jerusha's voice rasped.

Merry remained where she was, unspeaking and unmoving.

Jerusha crumpled the sopping handkerchief. "We're good workers. Never complain…" Her eyes had a dreamy quality to them as if she were speaking from a great distance.

Merry covered Jerusha's hand with her own, wanting to anchor her somehow.

Jerusha pulled away as if the contact hurt. "I see now how hate can crawl into a person's heart. It just finds the cracks from where it's been broken." She turned her face away, returning her gaze to the window. Desperation gleamed in her eye, and she gripped Merry's arm in talon-like fingers. "I can't lose him."

Merry rose on her knees until she was face-to-face with Jerusha. "You've told me that God works everything to good. You hold on to that. In the meantime, we have to think."

"Think about what?"

"I've heard that the Quakers of Pennsylvania have no heart for slavery."

Jerusha sat back as if she had been slapped. "What are you saying?"

Merry hardly knew herself. It was mad, impossible. Dangerous. For a moment the words wedged in her throat, too treacherous to be allowed voice. She thought of the children sobbing in the nursery, and the words spilled out of their own volition. "Take Daniel and run away."

A jolt of the cart nearly knocked Merry from her perch. She clutched at the seat and the precious parcel of medicines as she righted herself, but not before her wild gaze caught sight of a familiar face. She shook her head. Mayhap she was going mad. Graham Sinclair could not possibly be in Williamsburg.

But surely there could not be another such as he. His features had burned themselves into her memory with the intensity of a branding iron on a convict's thumb. His russet hair and dark eyes had been designed to melt an impressionable girl's heart. Hers had never stood a chance; and indeed, she had never attempted to guard it from him, but had welcomed his friendship and hoped for more.

When she was twelve and had found a bird with a broken wing in the garden, he had helped her tend it, and thus had sealed his heroic stature in her eyes. He had been Jason of the Argonauts, Sinclair the Great, and William the Conqueror rolled into one. She had believed him infallible and conformed every thought and opinion so that it mirrored his. At least, until he had abandoned her to care for her ailing father by herself, and then condemned her in his courtroom.

Merry blinked away the memories. She couldn't have seen him; therefore, it had just been nerves. She had a great deal to do, much of which could land her back in gaol for abetting a runaway. She pushed away thoughts of a phantom to focus on the task at hand.

In the morning she would claim that Jerusha and Daniel had come down with scarlet fever and insist they be quarantined in one of the outbuildings. She would see them away and keep up the pretense of treating them over the next week or so. Then she would pretend to discover their absence. That ought to give them plenty of time to evade a search party.

She inhaled deeply and nodded to herself. It should work.

It *would* work.

It had to.

Sunset splashed the city with the day's leftover color as the cart rattled up behind the mansion. The white walls glowed pink and orange, looking as if the house were blushing at some indiscretion.

She couldn't find it in her to pray for her own predicament, but for Jerusha… What could it hurt? *Lord, help Jerusha and Daniel. Help them to be free.*

Chapter 4

Graham grabbed Connor's arm and pointed. "That was Merry!"

Connor squinted after the open cart. "Yep."

In a trice they were sprinting after the cart. She was in his sights. He could not let her slip away again. He dodged a strolling couple and landed ankle deep in one of the puddles of wastewater that punctuated the street. It would be a miracle if he could salvage his boots. No matter. If the expense of a pair of boots was all it took to shift the weight of guilt this very night, he would pay it and gladly.

The cart turned and he lost sight of it. Redoubling his pace he swung around the corner with Connor hard on his heels. His side began to ache, and he gasped for breath. He pushed on in dogged pursuit, but the trotting cart horses were outpacing him.

He straggled to a walk when the cart turned down a street

lined with prosperous homes. He turned and found Connor a few paces behind him.

Breathless, hands on his knees, he gasped, "I think it's safe to assume that they must be going home." A laugh burbled up from his belly. "I can't think why I was in such a rush to follow."

Connor mopped his face. "I can." The big bruiser's mouth turned down, but then the laugh he had repressed bounced to the surface.

Graham put a hand on Connor's shoulder and bent over, laughing and trying to catch his breath. "Connor, you are supposed to keep me from being ridiculous."

"No man can make water run uphill."

"You wound me, brother. You wound me."

"Not mortally. You look thoroughly disreputable."

Graham glanced down at himself and realized the truth of it. His boots and breeches were splashed with effluvia from the street. His shirt was soaked through with perspiration and his neckcloth hopelessly disarranged.

Ought he return to his lodging for a change of linen? He could not bear the thought. His goal was within his grasp. In the brief glimpse he had of Merry, she had looked distinctly solemn. What if she suffered ill-use in that fine mansion? Could he live with himself if he allowed it to go on a moment more than necessary? He groaned. There was no way he was turning back at this point. He would see his task completed this very evening. "Come on."

Together they marched down the quiet street and turned in at the Benning gate. He had decided that he should tell Merry first, so he went around to the back entrance, where it would be more acceptable for a servant to receive someone. He raised his hand to knock, but hesitated, licking his lips.

"You want me to do this?" Connor stood at his elbow as always, supporting him by his mere presence.

Graham inhaled and knocked. "No."

A dignified black man answered the door, and Graham summoned a weak smile. "I would like to speak to Merry Lattimore."

The children were sleeping soundly by the time Merry returned from the apothecary. She went out to the kitchen for a bite of supper.

Cookie greeted her with a wave of her spoon. "Hello, Merry. Glad yer back, child. There's ham in the vittles today."

Merry bent over the pot. "Mmm, smells good." She heaped a pile into a bowl. "To what do we owe the honor?"

"Company. Mr. Benning's shipping partner, Mr. Fraser, is up from Charles Towne for a visit."

"Merry?"

Merry glanced up to find Mr. Benning's man, Isaiah, standing at the base of the stairs. "Isaiah, is everything well?"

"Yes ma'am. You have a visitor."

Unreasoning panic hit her like a punch. Who could it be? Had someone gotten wind of her plan? It wasn't possible. She hadn't even begun to act on it.

"Do you know who it is?"

"Mr. Sinclair—says he's a magistrate."

Merry slumped back onto the stool, face and hands suddenly clammy. "That is impossible. He's in London." Her words came out as a raspy whisper.

"He claims it's urgent."

"I have no wish to see him." Pushing to her feet she hurried from the kitchen.

Graham smiled and stepped forward as the manservant returned to the door. He had his hat half-off when the man held up a hand.

"I'm afraid Merry does not wish to see you."

"Pardon?"

"If I may say so, she seemed upset."

Graham merely blinked, hand suspended in the act of removing his hat. This could not be happening. It was simply too ridiculous. He had come halfway around the world to tell the minx that he had obtained her pardon, and she would not deign to see him?

The servant stepped back and the door shut firmly in Graham's face.

He whipped his hat the rest of the way off and ran a hand through his hair. Crushing the hat in his other hand, he slapped it against the doorframe.

"This is insufferable!"

Connor's lips were compressed in a manner that suggested he might be restraining a laugh. "Why don't you just mail the blooming papers, and I'll go book passage for home?"

Graham clapped his hat back on his head and stepped away from the door. "What we are going to do is set watch on this house until Merry Lattimore steps foot outside, and once she does, I am going to slap these papers in her hand and then bid her adieu and a pleasant life."

Merry tossed on her pallet bed until she thought she might go mad. What was Graham doing here? He belonged in London, pronouncing judgment on the masses. Or possibly at some country home, courting a squire's daughter. He belonged anywhere but here.

She put her hands to her cheeks, feeling the heat. She closed her eyes. Oh, there had been a day when she had longed for his arrival—waited, watched for it like an eager puppy. Nose pressed to the windowpane, her eyes had roamed over the foot traffic in the street. Watching, watching for a tall, lithe form in a bottle green coat and buff breeches. Russet hair tied back with a neat black ribbon. Dark, playful eyes that made her stomach flop like a landed fish.

Her fingertips brushed cool glass, reaching toward him when at last he appeared. She whirled to bound down the stairs in greeting only to find her mother standing in the doorway of her room.

"This will not do."

"What?"

"Flinging yourself after Mr. Sinclair in such a profligate manner."

Her cheeks ached as if they had been pinched a thousand times. Humiliation pulsing dull and sharp at the same time. "I just want to see him. He has been away so long."

"You haven't the sense of a nanny goat. Ladies do not wish to see men. Men wish to see us. I have told you this before."

"But—"

"Now, remember yourself, and for once act as a lady."

Mother ushered her from her room and down to the drawing room, a stiff hand on Merry's back both propelling her forward and restraining her. She took her place on the settee, hands gripping her embroidery hoop, but she couldn't make a stitch. Her eyes brimmed with tears, blurring the colored thread like a chalk drawing in the rain.

The door opened and Father ushered Graham in. Despite the weight of her mother's disapproval, Merry couldn't resist looking up, seeking his eyes. His delighted smile lit a glow in her, melting the reserve her mother's chilly words had iced around her heart.

She thrust aside her sewing and rushed to him, hands outstretched. They had a lovely afternoon.

And then he had never returned.

Father's health had begun to decline, and Graham disappeared, taking with him her hopes of love.

Merry started awake and pressed her fingers against her eyes. She had to find a way to banish these memories.

Abigail Benning had given her leave to borrow books from the library. Mayhap now was the time to avail herself of the privilege. Anything would be preferable to dwelling on her hurts or basking in dread of the errand she would have to perform that evening.

She slipped from the nursery and downstairs. The door to the parlor stood open, and conversation and laughter spilled out into the hallway.

She started to slip past, but the sound of her name brought her up short.

"Merry, we were just speaking of you, please come meet everyone."

She closed her eyes briefly. She had been so close. Straightening her spine, she turned back and entered the brightly lit drawing room. "Yes madam?"

Mrs. Benning sat next to a handsome youth. The lad was well formed with an unmistakable air of the master about him. Indeed, Mr. Benning must have looked just like him as a young man. Abigail patted the lad's arm. "This is Raleigh, my eldest son. He's been visiting with our friends the Frasers these many months. I'm so very happy to have him home." Her smile was brighter than the lamps that lit the room.

Another well-dressed couple sat among the family circle.

"And this is Mr. and Mrs. Fraser. They are good friends and partners with our family."

Mr. Benning hung back, standing behind the settee. A smile turned up the corners of his mouth, but it was as stiff and artificial as wooden flowers. Unlike the others who looked at her as if she were a performing monkey, his troubled gaze rested on Mr. Fraser.

Merry jerked her attention back to what Mrs. Benning was saying.

"Merry has proven to be a most adept stillroom maid. I don't know what I would have done without her help this past month."

Mr. Benning raised his glass. "To Merry Lattimore and her physics."

The fine folk raised their cups and laughed, tossing off the drinks in a go. Merry resisted the urge to smooth her apron.

Mrs. Benning embraced Master Raleigh again. "The children will be so pleased to see their brother if they are awake still."

"I'm sorry, madam, they were fatigued and went to sleep directly. Do you wish me to rouse them?"

Mrs. Benning looked to her son then shook her head. "No, I suppose not. He will see them in the morning."

The conversation swirled on, and Merry slipped away unnoticed. Thank goodness she had not been asked to wake the children. It would have been a battle to get them to sleep again. And she had plans for the evening.

Her fingers trembled at the thought of sneaking away in the night. At least the presence of guests meant that Mrs. Benning would be less likely to check on the children every few minutes as she had been wont to do in the past few days.

Merry selected a book at random from the library and returned to the refuge of the nursery. When at long last the rustles and murmurs faded into the quiet of night, she cracked open the nursery door and slipped into the hall.

A floorboard creaked, and she flattened herself into the shadow below the curve of the stairs. Master Raleigh stomped from his father's study, his face a study in scowling frustration.

Back pressed against the wall, she could feel his heavy tread reverberate through the house, just as his displeasure reverberated through the atmosphere.

Merry glanced at the front door. She was so close, and yet,

what if someone discovered her absence? They could add time to her sentence, or even tie her to the whipping tree. Her heart stuttered at the thought. She closed her eyes. Why must she always borrow trouble?

Then she pictured Jerusha's red-rimmed eyes as she stared out the window into nothingness. She owed Jerusha a great deal, and she had promised herself that she would never sit back idly while injustice prevailed.

Licking her lips, Merry crept from the safety of the deep shadows. There would be no return.

It was time to hie himself home. Darkness had long since fallen, and Graham was beginning to fear he would fall asleep in his discreet vantage point. It was too late for Merry to stir tonight. He would return in the morning to renew the watch.

He stood and pushed his fists into the small of his back. By his count, and he had counted it over several times in the last few hours, they were nearly even. True, she had been wrongly transported, but she had caused him almost enough trouble to make up for it. The thought of the feather tick awaiting him rose in his mind. It was most certainly time to head for bed.

A tiny creak drew his attention. He turned in time to see a small figure slip into the street. He knew that frame. Moonlight crawled from behind a cloud to illuminate her delicate features. What was she up to?

Graham hurried from the shadows to follow. Merry paused every so often as if to get her bearings, but she always started again, aiming for some, as yet unknown, goal. Had she some tryst planned? Or perhaps she was trying to sneak aboard a boat headed back to England. Pure folly. Any convict caught returning before they'd completed their term faced an automatic death sentence.

She skirted the market green and entered another area of residences and shops. Then around the edge of the College of

William and Mary and into a district chockablock with gin pits, gambling dens, and bawdy houses. At last she stopped in front of a tall, thin house. A porch lined each floor, but only on the side of the house, making it look like a debutante glancing coyly over her shoulder.

Merry approached the house and knocked on the door. It opened, and after a moment she was admitted. What could the girl be about?

He slipped into the narrow alley between a chandler's shop and a cartwright's paddock and settled in for another wait. He would find out what she was up to if it killed him.

Merry ought to have worn a cloak. Though ostensibly a private home, Sarah's business was all too public to risk being seen here.

At last the manservant who had admitted her returned and motioned her up the stairs. "Mistress Proctor will see you."

She followed him and was led into a small sitting room. Sarah rose to greet her. "Merry! It seems an age since I have had the pleasure of your company."

Merry embraced her friend and smiled. "You are looking well."

Indeed, she was. Gone was the gaudy dress she'd worn in Newgate. The gown she wore now was undoubtedly costly, but much more demure. And adorned by a single necklace of good quality. Her hair was piled high in an elaborate coiffure designed to show off her long, graceful neck. Everything about her bespoke taste and refinement.

"You tutored me well. And this new world has proven most lucrative. I may stay even after my term has expired. Come and sit. I must know how you are faring."

"I've come to beg a favor."

"Name it. I'm mistress here, and if it's in my power you shall have it."

"I need to borrow fifteen pounds."

Whatever Sarah had expected, this was not apparently it. Her eyebrows flew up in astonishment.

Merry rushed on. "I offer myself as surety. If I do not repay the debt, I shall indenture myself to you, though I must beg you to wait until my term of service with the Bennings is completed."

"What trouble have you found that you need such funds?"

Should she tell? Sarah knew as much about bondage as anyone. "A friend of mine is in desperate straits. Master Benning intends to sell off her son."

"Are you proposing to buy him? Fifteen pounds shan't prove sufficient."

Merry shook her head.

"Then what?" Eyes narrowed, Sarah stepped back, looking Merry over as if she did not know her. When her eyes reached Merry's face for the second time, she gasped and raised a hand to her mouth. "You intend to help them run away, don't you?"

Merry said nothing.

Her friend gripped her arm and leaned in close. "Are you mad? If you are caught… They do not treat such matters lightly here."

"I know."

Sarah's gaze searched her face. "I suppose if I don't agree to aid you in your folly, you will simply find some other means to obtain the funds?"

"You know me too well." Despite her weariness, Merry smiled.

Sarah shook her head. She looked as if she were about to refuse.

"I would not ask it for myself, Sarah. Please, I cannot sit by and see this boy torn from his mother. They… I must do this."

Sarah closed her eyes, her shoulders sagging. "You shall

have what you ask, but"—she clutched both Merry's hands in hers—"I beg you to be careful."

"I swear I will be."

Sarah gazed into her eyes, searching for something. A promise that all would be well, perhaps. Merry could offer no such pledge. Matters had gone awry for her all too frequently.

Her friend pulled away. "I'll be back in a moment."

Merry sank onto the settee, absently caressing the smooth arm. The satiny finish glowed in the candlelight. Everything about this house and its furnishings spoke of luxury. Sarah's dubious profession had at least provided the means to live well. Merry could not begrudge her success, and yet how was it that Sarah had prosperity and independence, while Merry's struggle to do right had landed her in naught but trouble?

Sarah returned with a small leather purse.

"Here it is, in silver. They wouldn't be able to pass off gold without being questioned. As it is there could be difficulties. Hard currency is not easily obtained in these colonies."

Merry stood and took the weight in her hands. "Thank you."

"Won't you reconsider?"

"I wish I could."

"Then take it, and do as you will." Sarah sounded petulant as she placed a hand on Merry's shoulder. "I'll pray for you."

Merry could not quite prevent her eyebrows from leaping for her hairline. "You will pray for me?"

Sarah grinned and gave her a push. Her old accent snuck into her voice. "Even if He don't take much notice of baggage like me, I figure it won't do any 'arm."

Merry hugged her. "I must go before I'm missed. Take care of yourself."

"And you."

Merry slipped back down the stairs and out the door. The weight of the purse made her feel conspicuous. If it should be stolen… Summoning her courage, Merry breathed a prayer. She really ought to have brought a cloak, and to the devil with the rain.

She tiptoed down the porch steps and out to the street, one hand on the purse to keep the coins from jangling. She knew the way now though. It oughtn't take long to get home.

A parcel of black-gowned students from the college swung around the corner, and she darted into an alley. The boisterous pack launched into a drinking song. Window sashes clattered open, and sleeping householders hurled invectives. One of the disgruntled neighbors may have thrown something, too, judging from the loud grunt and slurred guffaws.

Merry shivered in her hiding place and wrinkled her nose. With her usual good sense, she had hidden next to someone's privy. She sighed and willed the inebriated scholars to pass on. At last they did so, and she emerged into the street.

A misty rain crowded in, both miserably wet and curiously dry. Merry hunched forward. She'd be lucky to survive this night's outing. Water leached into her shoes, turning her feet clammy. The soles had been worn through since arriving in Virginia, and she had not the funds to replace them, or was that the Bennings' duty?

It did not matter at the moment. All that mattered was that the water from the streets was soaking through her stockings. She shivered. Behind her she heard the sound of another step.

Her heart skipped a little as if encouraging her to speed up. Suddenly cold in addition to wet, she sped up to a trot.

There it was again. Was someone following her or merely traveling in the same direction? Again, Merry picked up her pace, hurtling through the narrow streets in search of sanctuary.

A hand gripped her shoulder. She opened her mouth to scream.

Chapter 5

"Merry, it's me."

Strangling the cry for help, Merry turned to face Graham Sinclair. He loomed above her in the night, tall and lean. Handsome face clean and gleaming, his hair neatly tied behind with a black bow. If he had the sense of a gnat, he would fear her. She curled her fingers into her skirts to keep from striking him.

"Why are you skulking about so late at night?" she demanded.

"I could ask the same of you."

He held up a hand. "Miss Lattimore, I know I must not appear to be your greatest friend, but I have been working diligently on your behalf."

"Oh yes, I know." Her nostrils flared as if she smelled something even worse than Newgate. "You saw me committed to the blackest hole in England, with nothing to look forward to but death."

The force of her anger scored his brow with deep ridges. "Miss Lattimore, I did no more than my duty."

"Have you come to gloat then? I confess I do not understand it. My family and I were ever kind to you."

His other hand joined the first in a placating gesture, though his voice grew harsh. "I had no choice in the matter. The evidence against you was too strong."

Her skin flamed beneath his scrutiny. Clinging to the tail of her anger, she held her arms out wide as if modeling a new gown. "Allow your eyes to drink their fill. I have been brought low by the Pagets and your false sense of duty. I hope you are proud of all you have accomplished."

She could see the bob of his Adam's apple despite his stock.

The furnace of humiliation churning within her made even her eyes burn. He stepped back. His outstretched palms made him appear a supplicant. "I have no interest in seeing you brought low. Indeed, I owe your father too much for me to rejoice at your plight. I came to Virginia to find you."

"Surely you didn't assume I would desire your acquaintance after all that transpired. And why would you wish mine? I am nothing but a thief to you."

"Quiet." Graham held a finger to his lips. "Are you trying to draw the attention of the watchmen?"

She turned on her heel. "I did not desire this conversation at all. You accosted me."

"I know you didn't steal the jewels."

It was perhaps the only thing that could have made her stop and turn back. "You know?"

"Near the end of May the jewels turned up missing again. Upon investigation it was discovered that Lucas Paget had stolen them. It seems he was also the one to place them in your valise."

"Did he hate me so much?"

"It seems he feared you would tell his mother of his gambling debts."

Merry shook her head. "His debts? Surely, she already knew?"

"Not their full extent, I think."

"Do you mean to say that he purposely made it appear as if I had stolen those gems in order to discredit anything I might have told his mother?"

Graham shrugged.

She inhaled, fighting down a rage that stole her breath and blinded her. How could anyone be so depraved? So…so heedless of how their actions injured another person? She reached for a nearby wall to anchor herself. White-hot energy pulsed through her. The way she felt at the moment she could swim back to England and administer the thrashing Paget deserved.

Graham stepped closer. His eyes held a depth of understanding that prodded at her vitals. She closed her eyes against his sympathy. Despite herself she had been trying to salvage some sort of meaning from the madness. But no. It had all been senseless. A tragic waste. She shook off the gentle hand he placed on her arm and bared her teeth in a snarl.

"Have you come all this way to tell me that I'm innocent?"

"No." He whipped off his hat and ran a hand through his hair. "I've come because I have obtained a pardon for you."

"What?" Merry took a step back. The world spun and contracted.

"When I discovered the truth I petitioned the king and obtained a pardon."

"You did that for me?"

"Contrary to what you seem to think, I believe in justice and honor."

Tears stung her eyes. "I do not know what to think."

"You used to think me a friend." His voice was as gentle

as the mist. He opened his jacket and pulled out an oilskin-wrapped packet, which he extended toward her.

Merry took it in trembling fingers. Home. She could go home. She could not speak. Tears spilled over onto her cheeks. Mayhap they would mix with the rain and he would not notice in the dark.

"Everything you need should be in there. If you wish, I will come to the Benning home tomorrow and explain it all. They may not want to let you go after having paid for you."

She opened her mouth to thank him when a sick feeling settled in her stomach. If she left the Bennings now, there would be no way she could help Jerusha and Daniel. Her hands began to tremble. "That will not be necessary."

The weight of the money pouch tugged at the waist of her skirt. She could forget that any of this had ever happened. Just book passage on the next ship leaving Virginia.

Graham was looking at her with an intensity that unnerved her. Could the man read her mind? She cast about for a means of explaining her reluctance. "They have been very good to me. Once they see the documents they will be just."

He gazed down at her, searching her face. "Are you certain? It would pain me a great deal to have gone to all this trouble and then for you to remain trapped here."

"By all means we must be certain that you are spared any pain."

He pulled back, the moon glinting on the hurt in his eyes.

Merry swallowed hard. "I'm sorry. I ought not to have said that. But I prefer to handle this matter myself."

"Then I bid you adieu." Stiffly he turned away.

"Mr. Sinclair?"

"Yes?"

"I… Thank you. You have accomplished something I never dreamed possible."

He stepped back to her side and took her hand in his. "Miss

Lattimore, I am so dreadfully sorry for all that has befallen you, and for my part in it."

The warmth of his hand encircling hers sent a shiver up her spine. She looked up, searching his face, but shadows hid his eyes.

"My father said you had the most finely honed sense of honor he ever encountered."

He chuckled. "Of late, it has caused me a great deal of trouble." He took her hand and laid it on his bent arm. "Please allow me to see you back to the Benning house." He made no move to lead her away.

Merry could not seem to move or even to tear her gaze away from his. Almost dreamily he raised a hand and cupped her cheek. "You've not been harmed, have you?"

"No."

"You relieve my mind greatly." As if suddenly realizing the inappropriateness of his proximity he turned and strolled with her as if they were on the Strand in London rather than the backwater of Williamsburg.

The loss of his warmth was a kind of bereavement, but Merry attributed her desire for closeness to the chill of the rain.

Her foot slipped in something thick and viscous, and the coins in Sarah's pouch clanked. He glanced at her sharply but didn't comment, and she chose not to explain. It was not his affair. He would likely interfere if she confided in him. What he did not know, he could not divulge.

"Mrs. Paget's lady's maid, Grace, gave me your valise. I have it in my lodgings. Will you receive me if I bring it to you tomorrow?" His playful tone covered a wounded note.

It was Merry's turn to ignore what she did not wish to confront. "You've seen Grace? How was she? I was so concerned when I left."

"She seemed hale and hearty. I doubt any of them were surprised to see Lucas Paget come to a bad end."

He fulfilled her desire for news from England, describing every detail he could recall of his interviews with the Pagets' servants. He even made her laugh as he described Lucas's ignominious arrest.

Merry would never have dreamed that she would find herself in such a situation, and yet here she was, walking in the rain in the middle of the night with Graham Sinclair, and nearly enjoying herself.

Having reached the Benning home, Merry left Graham at the gate and continued on alone. She slipped in the same door she had left by and bolted it behind her. She crept up the stairs. No one stirred, though she thought she saw the gleam of Daniel's eyes as she passed his pallet in the hall.

She breathed more easily once she slipped into the nursery. Hastily she hid Sarah's purse and the documents regarding her pardon.

Then she gladly changed out of her wet dress and donned a dry nightgown. She towel dried her hair and lay down on her pallet. It felt so good to lie flat. She stretched out and sighed, listening to the rain that had picked up pace until it drummed in steady cadence against the roof.

In just a few days this would all be over, and she could go home to England. She practiced saying it aloud. "England."

Somehow the notion had become ephemeral, as difficult to conceive as the drops of water in the ocean. She shifted on her pallet, kneading the straw inside into more comfortable lumps.

Despite the chill in the air, she broke into a sudden sweat. No. Oh no. What had she done? In borrowing money for Jerusha, she had offered herself as surety. It had all seemed so distant and tenuous. Jerusha would have found the means to repay the debt before Merry's years of service were completed with the Bennings. But now…

Perhaps they could get by on less. It mightn't be as easy for them to escape, and especially for them to start a new life, but they were used to handling difficulties. Certainly they were more used to poverty than stewardship.

Merry rolled over again, the metallic taste of shame on her tongue.

Had exposure to crooks and ruffians robbed her of her sense of justice? And yet, what benefit had justice ever provided her? Why should she not grasp at her opportunity for freedom?

"To do justly, and to love mercy." As if in a hazy mirror, an image of her father's face rose to the forefront of her mind. She shook her head to banish the vision. He had loved to speak of ideals, but there were no ideal situations, only chasms of chance to be avoided. It seemed that if she did not fall into this one, there was another nearby, yawning wide to swallow her.

A rustle, a murmur, a clatter in the hall. Chewing on her lip guiltily, Merry sat up. She swept back the coverlet, tiptoed to the door, and opened it a scant few inches.

Jerusha stood in huddled conversation with Daniel on the other side. She glanced up as Merry peeked out. "Master's ill. Come quick."

Merry nodded and slipped through the door, as quietly as possible so as not to disturb the children.

A cluster of slaves and visitors stood in the hall outside the master's room. They opened a path for her, and she entered to find Abigail Benning clinging to her husband's hand. The room stank of the vomit that befouled the bedding and floor. Red welts splotched Mr. Benning's face and chest. He opened his mouth to speak, and his features contorted. Veins corded his neck and stood out in stark relief at his temples.

Tears streamed down Abigail's cheeks. "Help him, please." The terror in her eyes tugged Merry forward.

"We need to stop him from vomiting," Jerusha said.

His eyes rolled back in their sockets. "Angel." He reached a hand toward Merry.

"No." Merry put a hand on Abigail's arm to draw her attention from her husband's agony. "The vomiting is good. His body is trying to purge itself of some evil humor."

Abigail looked deeply into her eyes for a moment and then nodded. "Listen to what she says."

"Has a physician been summoned?"

Jerusha stepped forward. "I sent Daniel."

"Hattie, I need towels and water. Jerusha, I will need marshmallow."

Both slaves sped from the room, their skirts whipping up a breeze.

Merry took Mr. Benning's wrist, trying to find the speed of his pulse.

Harsh and pointed, the blood pounded through his vessels in angry surges. The skin was flushed and hot, and carmine blotches blossomed on his arms and hands. His eyes fluttered shut. She opened the lids to find they had rolled back in his head.

She had seen something like it once when her father had been summoned to tend to an emergency while they had been on an outing together. Surely this could not be the same thing? She shook her head.

Not poison.

Someone handed Merry the water and towels she had requested. She soaked one of the towels in the basin and wrapped it around the master's neck. She spoke soothingly and wiped the sweat from his forehead with another dampened towel.

Jerusha returned with an entire basket of medicinal herbs

from the garden, each labeled and preserved in its own paper packet. She had also thought to bring the mortar and pestle and the bloodletting kit from the stillroom.

"You are ahead of me, Jerusha. Thank you."

Jerusha took the towel from her hand. "I'll do this."

Merry met her gaze and nodded. "I need some lukewarm rose tea."

"I'll get it." Isaiah hurried from the room.

Merry flipped through the packets until she found the marshmallow. She unfolded the packet, tapped some into the mortar, and began to grind the dried leaves into powder.

The voices in the hall escalated in timbre.

Isaiah appeared at her side with a pitcher of tea.

She mixed a dose of powdered marshmallow into the tea. "Help me hold his head."

Jerusha and Isaiah held his head still as Merry put the cup to his lips and slowly tipped in a sip. He gurgled and gasped. His eyes popped open.

Abigail murmured soothing noises. The rigidity in his frame relaxed slightly when his gaze found her.

"Angel." Again that single strange word.

The night spun out in jerky starts, as if time were a spool of yarn fitfully unwound. The marshmallow seemed to curb the violence of the purging, but his pulse remained hard and driven. With Jerusha's help, Merry made a tincture of hawthorn and administered it.

Another shifting in the hall and Dr. de Sequeyra arrived. "What is this then?"

Abigail dissolved into incoherent tears.

The slaves pulled back, looking to Merry. She outlined the symptoms she had observed and the physic she had administered. "I had thought to bleed him, but the pulse was so forceful I feared he would lose more than necessary."

The dignified physician nodded and opened his bag. He

pulled out a lancet and scalpels. "Very right. He seems to be resting more comfortably now." He picked up his instruments and turned to the bed.

"The writhing has slowed," Merry said, racking her tired brain to provide all the details her father would have required in the same circumstance.

"You did well. Perhaps you could assist me further?"

"Yes sir. My father was a physician." She glanced up to find the good doctor regarding her approvingly.

He nodded directly. "See what you can do about relieving us of our audience."

Licking her lips, Merry did as she was bidden. Only Abigail refused to be shooed away. She stayed at her husband's side, never releasing her grip on his hand.

Dr. de Sequeyra kept Merry moving throughout the night as they fought for Reginald Benning's life. Somewhere around dawn, bloody spittle began to dribble from his mouth.

Merry quickly dabbed it away and glanced up to see if Abigail had seen.

They had lost.

By midmorning, he was dead.

The sun spread the town with a butter-colored glow. Graham led Connor around to the back entrance of the Benning home. He breathed in deeply, feeling a hundred pounds lighter. True, Merry hadn't initially reacted as he would have liked, but she had softened by the time he had seen her home. It wouldn't take long to convince her to return with him. It wasn't as if she had a great number of options at her disposal.

Merry's valise banged against his leg. The return of her things might even beguile a smile from her.

He knocked on the frame of the open door. Connor came up beside him, as stiff and alert as a bird dog on the scent.

Graham's smile withered as he took in a more careful account of the house and grounds.

Not one servant bustled through the exposed corridor. The house was silent, with neither the murmur of voices nor the clatter of activity.

His boot scraped the bricks, and he turned around. No one toiled in the garden nor drew water at the well. He knocked again, his knuckles stinging from the sharp blows.

A coltish young maid shuffled from a side hall, saw them at the door, and approached. Her eyes were red-rimmed. Her face haggard. "Yes sir?"

"I wish to speak to Merry Lattimore."

"Yes sir. Come in and wait if you please." She sounded infinitely weary.

Removing their hats, Graham and Connor followed her into the hall.

Heavy silence blanketed the house and muffled every other sense as well. Though it was approaching lunchtime he could smell nothing from the kitchen. And the curtains were drawn tightly shut in most every room, leaving the house in gloomy shadow. He and Connor exchanged a wary glance, but neither could bring themselves to shatter the odd quiet. What might they find lying beneath?

Merry descended a narrow back stairwell on silent, slipper-shod feet. The black smudges beneath her eyes and pallor of her features confirmed his worst suspicions.

"Miss Lattimore."

"Good afternoon, Mr. Sinclair. Thank you for bringing my things." She held her hand out for the bag.

What could have happened? He lowered his voice and stepped closer to her. "Is everything well?"

"Mr. Benning died this morning."

"Do you have a moment?"

"I must get back to the children. I dislike leaving them. They are understandably upset."

"Of course." Graham handed the valise over, feeling at loose ends. "Perhaps I might call on you later, to make sure you are well?"

She nodded listlessly. "As you wish." Once more her tone held almost no inflection. Was she struggling with grief... or fear?

The appearance of a constable in the drawing room nearly paralyzed Merry with the certainty that she would be dragged to gaol. Heart galloping, she pulled the children close.

She breathed deeply through her nose, trying to still the surge of anxiety. She would not crumble into helplessness. The children needed her and so did Mrs. Benning. Their world had overturned like a phaeton in a strong wind. They needed someone to comfort, not drain them of their few remaining resources.

"So sorry for your loss. A great gentleman." Tricorn in hand, the constable delivered condolences to the room at general.

"Thank you, Mr. Harold." Abigail motioned for the man to be seated. He did so after a moment's hesitation and a brief swipe at the back of his pants with one hand.

"Such a shocking loss. So sudden."

Abigail's delicate nostrils flared as if she were fighting back more tears. She managed to retain control, though the struggle turned her voice high and tight. "Yes it was." She tried to turn to business. "I am not certain yet when we will best be able to accommodate the inventory."

"Oh yes, ma'am, we will stay out of the way of the family. I thought I would ask Mr. Geddy to help, since I know little about shipping and whatnot."

"That seems prudent."

"Thank you, ma'am. Could you direct me to Dr. de Sequeyra? He asked to speak to me."

"I offered him the use of a guestroom so that he could wash and rest before riding home. Jerusha will show you the way."

"Thank you, ma'am." The constable dropped his hat and bent to pick it up with a quick, awkward motion. He backed from the room, head bobbing like a turkey's as he bade his farewell.

The sober, diminished conversation of a house in mourning resumed as the man left.

"I am glad we could be here with you at such a terrible time." Catherine Fraser reached a hand to pat Abigail's arm. "I cannot imagine how it would be to go through all this alone. I hope you will allow us to do all we can to help." Her darkly elegant gown and quiet voice were perfectly modulated to mourning.

"I am grateful to have good friends around at such a time." Abigail sounded weary beyond human endurance. Red-rimmed eyes set in a chalky white face seemed to burn through the conventions and reduce the others in the room to fumbling.

Mrs. Fraser rallied and tried again. "Mr. Fraser will manage the funeral of course. You oughtn't to worry with such matters. And of course, I can do whatever needs to be done to keep the household running smoothly."

Abigail stood, swaying slightly. "Would you excuse me please? I feel…unwell."

Merry stood and hurried to brace her. She looked over her shoulder. "Children, find Hattie, please, while I help your mama to her room."

Wide-eyed they nodded, fear patent in their swollen eyes.

"Excuse me, ma'am."

Everyone in the room turned to find the constable in the

door again. If possible he looked even more ill at ease, shifting from foot to foot, hands revolving his hat.

"Yes?" Abigail leaned more heavily into Merry as if the weight of trepidation were too much to bear.

"May I speak with you...privately?"

"Let us go into my closet." She took a step and reached back for Merry's hand, her grip as cold as a November fog. "Come with me, dear."

Safely ensconced in the small room where she handled household affairs, Mrs. Benning collapsed in a chair, and Merry stood beside her with a hand on her seat back assuring her of her presence and support.

"It's this way, ma'am. Dr. de Sequeyra found Mr. Benning's death a bit strange."

Mrs. Benning shook her head. "Strange?"

"He suspects poison."

Her features blanched even further. "What?"

The constable held up a hand. "Most likely it was an accident. This sort of thing happens. Something gets picked with the dinner herbs."

Abigail shook her head back and forth. "No. No. I'm... There must be some mistake."

"The doctor believes the illness was caused by lily of the valley. According to him it doesn't take long to take effect. I just need to interview the staff to see who picked it and how it got into your supper."

Merry frowned. "It was not in the supper or others would have been ill as well." The words sprang of their own accord from her lips. She winced and drew back a step as if she could distance herself from her own outspokenness.

The constable looked at her reproachfully, and even Abigail glanced up at her with lowered brows.

The constable sniffed and returned his attention to Abigail. "It might have been in any number of things. Dr. de Sequeyra says that even water from a vase that had held lilies would be enough to poison a man."

Abigail shook her head. "I don't recall picking any lilies recently."

The constable pushed his lips out in an exaggerated pucker. His head bobbed again in comedic fashion, though Merry felt no desire to laugh. "I'll need to speak to your cook and see what else Mr. Benning might have eaten, and who prepared it, and so on."

Tight little lines radiated around Abigail's mouth. "Do what you must." She rose. "I must see to my childr…"

Her hand reached for the chair but missed, and she swayed toward the fireplace.

Merry grabbed hold of her and guided her back down into the seat. "Pray wait here, ma'am. I'll fetch the doctor."

She shooed the constable before her and hurried in search of Dr. de Sequeyra. He prescribed immediate bed rest, and Mrs. Benning was bundled upstairs. Jerusha and Merry helped her out of the restrictive day dress she wore and into her nightdress. The doctor once again checked her pulse then administered a sleeping draught.

With Jerusha installed in silent vigil, Merry hurried in search of the children. She found them sitting mournfully in bed, their solemn little faces drained of their usual vitality. She checked them each for signs of returned fever. They seemed cool enough, despite their listlessness. When none of their toys captured their interest, she settled in to read to them.

They burrowed close, seeking the comfort of contact. Their innocent bewilderment broke her heart. They sensed the household's sorrow, but could not truly grasp the cause. They had never before been faced with such a loss. Her eyes stung with exhaustion and the dreadful dryness that remains when tears have been shed. Emma sighed. Nestling her head against Merry's arm, the rigidity in her little frame eased into the limpness of sleep. Merry stroked the girl's hair. She leaned her head back against the wall and allowed her eyes to drift closed.

The fire in the grate of her family's drawing room in London drew her close, and she stretched her hands toward it. She glanced at the clock on the mantel. Father would have been interred by now. Her tears hissed as they hit the hot bricks of the hearth.

The incessant snick of her mother's lace tatting needles grated against her nerves. Her self-satisfied conversation grated even more. "At least now you can marry Lord Carroll. He's been very gracious in not demanding your answer because of your father's illness."

Her jaw clenched against a rush of indignant words. "I have given him a response. More than once."

"Nonsense. You'll see differently now that your father is gone."

"I shall not." *The whispered words were nearly swallowed in the crackle of flames. Where, oh where, was Graham? Not a word, not a note from him in months. She had believed, hoped, that Graham loved her and would offer for her. But then he had disappeared at almost the same time Father had become so ill. Now Father was dead, and still he made no appearance. She would never have believed he would abandon her at the hour of her greatest need.*

"You shall, or you shall not have a dowry."

Merry whirled. "No, Mother! I will not marry that man. He is loathsome."

Her mother looked up from her lacework. She narrowed her eyes, a calculating gleam lending her a venal appearance. "You'll marry him, or you'll not stay under my roof another night."

She was running. Fleeing. Cold wind hurtled past her,

whipping her hair into tangles that blinded her. She stumbled. Fell.

Falling.

Merry jerked awake. A chilly breeze raised gooseflesh on her arms. Night had crept up on her. She rubbed at her eyes and then her temples where a dull throb pulsed. If only she could stretch out and sleep for a week.

Instead she slid carefully from between the still-sleeping children. Tenderly she tucked them under their coverlets. Blinking back tears she retrieved Emma's doll from the floor where it had fallen and settled it in the crook of the girl's arm.

In the kitchen, Cookie tended some sort of stew as it hung over the fireplace.

"Are you all right?"

Cookie spun around as if she had been branded. "Lands, you scared me."

"I'm sorry. I just wondered how you are faring."

Tearstains ravaged the older woman's face. "I never thought I'd see the day, and that's the truth. I can't hardly believe it."

Merry sat at the table. "He seemed so...invincible."

Cook's eyebrows drew together in a bemused frown. "I'm not talkin' 'bout the master. Everyone has to die sometime."

"Then wha—"

"They took Jerusha away. Said as how she murdered 'im."

Chapter 6

For the second night in a row, Merry slipped away from the house as the shadows sank into midnight. She'd learned her lesson and wore a cape with a hood that disguised her features. Better to have anonymity than the freshness of a breeze on her face.

Once again she fingered the scrap of paper on which she had scrawled the address. She could not afford to mistake her location.

Shadows shifted before her, deepening as she drew near. The rustle of desiccated leaves sounded as if a woman in bombazine was hard on her heels. Despite herself, Merry glanced over her shoulder.

She picked up her pace, scurrying through the heart of Williamsburg as if she were an escaped convict.

Perhaps she was.

From the bowels of the night she heard a scrape and scrambled for cover behind a rain barrel. She licked her lips as she crouched in the dark. A night watchman appeared around the corner swinging his lantern.

"One o'clock and all is well. Fair night out. No clouds to tell."

Merry leaned her forehead against the rough oak barrel. Her eyes slid closed and she sighed. Only the ache in her legs got her moving again. She swayed slightly as she rose, placing a hand on the barrel to steady herself. The faster she completed her errand, the faster she could get to bed.

She found the house and pulled her hood farther down to hide her features. Breathing deeply she rapped hard on the door. No sound stirred within. She tried again, pounding for a long moment.

At last a woman dressed in a wrapper and nightcap answered. She appeared frightened. "What is it?" she asked in a hiss.

"I must speak to Mr. Sinclair. It is urgent."

The woman glared at her through narrowed eyes. "Come back in the morning."

Merry had the presence of mind to shove her foot in the door. "Fetch him now."

"Get out before I call the watch."

"He has already passed. I apologize for the disruption, but if you wish to return to your slumber you would do well to call for Mr. Sinclair."

The woman stepped closer, outrage in her eyes. "Listen here—"

"Thank you, Mrs. Bartlesby, but I am awake."

The goodwife turned to the voice at the head of the stairs. "Do you know this…young person?"

"I do, and I am certain she would not disturb the household unless the matter was of great import." Looking somber, Graham appeared in the narrow slice of interior Merry could see. Worry lines framed his eyes.

"I assure you, it is," Merry said, removing her now bruised foot from the door.

The landlady harrumphed and departed for her bed.

Graham edged the door open. The concern in his eyes made Merry's heart stutter from its usual rhythm.

"If you have sought me out it must be a matter of dire concern."

"I don't know where else to turn." It was true. If this did not work... Merry's fingers pleated the edge of her apron as she awaited his verdict.

"Come in."

He led the way into a small drawing room and motioned for her to be seated. "I am sorry I have no refreshments to offer."

Merry shook her head. She continued to fold her apron between fidgety fingers. It would be best to be out with it. "The authorities believe Mr. Benning was poisoned."

"Poisoned?" Graham sat forward in his seat.

"At first they seemed to believe it was an accident, but later they took Jerusha into custody."

"Who is Jerusha?"

"A slave woman. My friend."

He waited.

"She had no reason to kill him."

"Then why do they believe she did?"

Unexpected tears stung Merry's eyes, and her breath caught in her throat. If she told him of their plans and he wrapped himself in his justice's robe, she could lose her freedom once again. All it would take was his word against hers just as with Lucas Paget. Could she face that fate?

She rubbed her burning eyes with trembling hands. If only she weren't so tired. Mayhap she had made a mistake coming here.

"Miss Lattimore." His gentle voice coaxed her to look at him. "Whatever you say I shall keep in confidence. But you must tell me what the trouble is so that I may help." His hand covered hers, warm and powerful.

She lifted her head to meet his gaze. Sincerity shone in his eyes, and something else, some deeper regard. A hint of the young man who had helped her bind a broken bird's wing so many years ago.

She swallowed and forced a tremulous smile. She had not been mistaken. "I know Jerusha did not kill Mr. Benning. They will say that she did it because he intended to sell her son away to a man from another colony. But we—*I* had a plan. I intended to help them escape. So you see, if she had another means of averting her worst fear, she would have no cause to take his life."

"You intended to abet a runaway slave?" Horror lanced his voice, reducing it to a sibilant hiss.

"The slaves of Virginia are no less people than anyone else, and yet they are reduced to mere chattel." Merry shook her head vehemently. "I have been so reduced, and I can tell you that humanity is lost more often when power over another is gained than the reverse."

He placed a finger under her chin and nudged it up until she met his gaze again. "I do not question your morals in this matter, only your sense. Do you realize how dangerous—"

Merry's spine straightened as if infused with iron. She jerked her chin from his gentle grip. "It was all planned and would have meant only a minimal amount of danger for me."

"You could be hanged. Must you tempt fate again?"

She scooted to the edge of her chair. "*I* tempt fate? The circumstances that led to my downfall were hardly of my manufacture."

"I did not imply it was your fault, simply that you should be careful."

"You act as if I have no acquaintance with the ways of the world, when it was through your 'kind' offices that I was locked in with every manner of wastrel and criminal. I may have been naive upon entering Newgate, but I was not so when I emerged from that school of vice."

Graham paled, his mouth drawing into a thin line. "I have done all in my power to remedy my mistake." The words were as sharply severed as if they had met with the guillotine.

Merry gritted her teeth. She had endured much greater insult than he had offered and hardly blinked an eye. She breathed deeply.

"I told you of our plans so you would understand that Jerusha had no cause to murder her master. She had found other means of solving her dilemma."

"And what do you wish me to do with this information?"

Was he determined to make this as difficult as possible? "I have come to ask you to represent Jerusha in the courts."

Surely he had been expecting such a thing? Yet he sat back with narrowed eyes.

"Do you seriously believe that a slave could use as her defense the notion that she intended to run away?"

Merry closed her eyes and looked down at her hands. "I—she did not—"

"I have never practiced law in this colony."

"Surely it cannot be so difficult. Nearly every lawyer in Williamsburg sat at the Middle Temple for instruction, just as you did." Her desperate hope was slipping away.

"I had intended to return to England on the first available packet."

Merry gritted her teeth. Time to discard her pride. "I beseech you, Mr. Sinclair. I know that Jerusha did not do what she is accused of. I also know how highly you prize the ideal of justice." She raised a hand to her stuttering heart. Perhaps a dash of guilt would help him to decide. She opened her mouth to remind him of the mistake he had made in her case.

But he spoke before she did. "You are correct. I love justice." He offered her a rueful smile. "I am also coming to value mercy. I will speak to Jerusha, but…"

Merry held her breath and met his gaze steadily.

"You must understand that this will not be easily settled."

"I understand that Jerusha will die unless someone does something to help her."

He rubbed his face wearily. "I shall undertake to see her tomorrow."

He looked so worn that Merry softened. She placed a tentative hand on his sleeve, feeling the warmth of him through linen and brocade. "Thank you." The words came out close to a whisper. "This means a great deal to me. More than I can say."

"Tell me all you know." His free hand covered hers as it rested on his arm, his gaze seared hers with a look at once unfathomable and unguarded. A scalding flush rose through her neck and into her cheeks. She caught her breath.

At last she could bear the weight of his regard no longer and pulled her hand from beneath his.

She cleared her throat, making an effort to sound normal. Carefully she recounted all she could of Mr. Benning's illness and all that had been done to save him.

Graham proved a good listener. His questions incisive. "Who brought the medicines?"

"Jerusha."

"Is it possible she tampered with them?"

"There wasn't time. And besides, he had already been poisoned, though I did not wish to think it at the time."

"How was the diagnosis of poison made?"

"I cannot answer for Dr. de Sequeyra, but it occurred to me almost immediately. Mr. Benning was covered by a virulent red rash. And he said the word *angel* twice. That combined with the intensity of his pulse and vomiting called to mind a case my father treated." Despite the gravity of the discussion, Merry almost smiled. Her mother would have been appalled to hear this conversation. And yet Graham seemed not so squeamish. Perhaps all her mother's pronouncements had been her own opinion, and not truly representative of his feelings at all. He seemed genuinely interested in her opinion—in this matter at least.

"Why the word *angel*?"

"The toxin in lily of the valley can cause a person to see a halo around objects or people."

"When was it administered?"

Merry stared into the fire. "I don't know. It would not take long for the poison to act. It must have been shortly before he went to bed."

"Did Jerusha have opportunity to dispense the poison?"

Merry swallowed and then nodded. "She took both Mr. and Mrs. Benning their evening's draught each night before bed."

Graham sighed and sat back in his seat. "Matters are not promising. Jerusha had the means and the opportunity to commit this murder."

"I swear she did not. She would not. As I told you, we had it all planned."

He held up a quieting hand. "We must face the realities if we are to overcome them. Your own case might have been decided differently if you had understood the weight of the evidence against you."

She could scarce argue with that. "What do you intend? I checked. We have only three days before the hustings court convenes."

"I shall ask questions. Luckily, my friend Connor has accompanied me, and I will enlist his aid. I swear to you that I will do everything in my power to absolve her. You can return to England in peace, knowing you have done all you can in aid of your friend."

Merry cocked her head. "I have no intention of proclaiming my innocence until this matter has been resolved."

He stiffened and frowned, eyebrows drawing together. "Whyever not?"

She clenched her jaw. This was more like the Graham Sinclair she'd known of late. "I have grown fond of the children and of Mrs. Benning. They do not need more upheaval in their lives at this time. And besides, if Jerusha did not kill Mr. Benning, someone else did. Surely the most effective means of proving Jerusha's innocence is to discover who is guilty. I am perfectly placed in the household to search for evidence of the true killer."

"This is far too dangerous." He stood. "I forbid it."

Merry stood as well. "You can forbid me nothing. You are not my guardian."

He sighed heavily. "Don't be fatuous. Investigation is dangerous work. If you intend to go through with this, then perhaps I shall withdraw as Jerusha's counsel."

Merry shrugged out of her cloak and draped it over one arm, her chill gone. "Then it is even more imperative that I discover who really committed the murder. And I shall start with Mr. Fraser."

He ran a hand through his hair. "Then I shall be forced to present myself to Mrs. Benning and inform her of your good fortune myself."

She breathed in through her nose. Once. Twice. "I don't think you would do anything so ridiculous. You are more a gentleman, and more intelligent, than that. But if you do, I will destroy the proofs and claim not to know you, and you shall look like an imbecile."

Chin high, Merry managed to sweep from the house before she began to cry. It was no wonder he had never married. Who could bear with such a manner?

* * *

Grumbling under his breath, Graham shrugged out of his robe. Drat the chit. There were times she had not the sense of a goat. Hadn't he already warned her of the dangers of walking about at night? She had either the hardest head in Williamsburg or the thickest.

He had no time to go upstairs in search of his boots. And yet there was something valiant about her heedless courage. Sighing, he slipped from the house, taking care to secure the door behind him.

There was no fathoming women. He scanned the street searching for a hint of her passing. Which direction had she taken? In fact, how had she found him in the first place? The situation seemed to sum her up, a bundle of competence and naïveté.

He set off in the direction that would lead most directly to the Benning house. Trotting in double time he soon spied a small figure ahead of him. It could only be Merry. He picked up his pace until he was no more than a block behind. He opened his mouth to call out, but thought better of it. No woman would want her name heralded through town in the middle of the night. Come to think of it, after her tantrum, it might be best to lag behind and simply watch to make certain she made it home.

A shadow disengaged from its brothers and lurched toward Merry.

Graham sprang forward. A yell as savage as an Indian war cry tore from his throat.

The shadow reached for her. Snatched at her shoulder and spun her around. Sprinting, Graham tucked in his chin and lowered his shoulder to barrel into the attacker.

His shoulder hit naught but air, but his knee and shin caught on something that sent him tumbling. He threw out his hands to catch himself, grunting at the bite of gravel against his palms. In clumsy haste he rolled over, prepared to parry an attack.

But no attack followed. The only sound was a low groan. A man knelt in the street rocking slightly, his shoulders hunched.

Well, that explained what he had tripped over, but what in heaven had happened?

Merry stood over him, her face as fierce as an avenging angel in the moonlight. The light of recognition dawned, and her hands dropped to her sides.

Graham sat up. "What did you do?"

"Something my friend Sarah taught me." She looked smug as she offered him a hand up. "What are you doing?"

"I'm picking gravel from my palms. You might have warned a fellow."

"I meant why are you here?"

"I followed to make sure no harm came to you."

If possible she looked even smugger. "As you can see I am perfectly well."

"I see." He squinted at her. Mayhap there was less naïveté in her makeup than he had guessed. "Do you know this fellow? Do you wish to call the watch?"

The smugness fled, to be followed by wide-eyed horror. "Heavens no. I don't wish to be found out of the house this evening."

He clambered to his feet. Eyes still narrowed, he offered his arm. "I've come this far, perhaps you would not mind if I saw you home."

After a moment's hesitation she accepted. "As you wish, but we cannot make a habit of this."

Graham looked over his shoulder to find the dark figure still crumpled like a dirty handkerchief. He nodded and restrained the desire to administer a good kick of his own.

Merry flicked a sidewise glance up at him. "Are you wearing house slippers?"

Despite himself he flushed. "I did not want to miss catching you."

She shook her head, but the caustic comment he expected did not emerge. "I appreciate your concern."

This was his chance to repair the offense he had caused. "It was the same impulse that prompted my earlier remarks. I care for your safety, though perhaps I could express it in a less heavy-handed fashion."

"That would be a pleasant change. If you think you can manage it."

Ah, there was the biting repartee.

He halted, drawing her to a standstill as well, and offered his best bow. "I can but try. Perhaps you will do me the honor of keeping me humble? You are so good at it."

She turned her face away, but not before he caught the ghost of a smile flicker across her features.

Chapter 7

Merry woke to find herself wedged between two small bodies. Sometime in the night the children had climbed from their beds to cuddle on her pallet. Dried tearstains still streaked John's downy cheeks. She traced the path with the pad of her thumb. Poor baby.

He sighed in his sleep and turned on his side. Gently, Merry edged from between the children and stood. What she wouldn't give for a few more minutes of sleep. Temptation pulled at her as inexorably as gravity. She yawned. Stretched. There was much to be done.

Yawning again, she coiled her hair up and covered it with her mobcap. In a few moments she was in the kitchen inquiring about breakfast for the children.

The other slaves had already eaten, and Hattie was in the scullery, so she found herself alone with Cookie. Merry stood with her bowl of mush and watched her for a moment. Despite her age, the old slave woman moved about her tasks with economical grace.

"Cookie?"

"Yes, honey?" She scarcely looked up from the dough she was kneading.

"You don't think Jerusha did this, do you?"

Cookie stopped then and studied her for a long moment. "No." She returned to pummeling the dough. "No, I don't."

"Then someone else must have."

"Don't know nothing 'bout that." She stared doggedly at the dough she worked.

"What do you know of the Frasers?"

"Nothin' I ain't already told you."

Merry put her palms flat on the worktable. "They're the only newcomers to the household. Unless someone else came to see Mr. Benning late in the evening." She reached a tentative hand out to touch Cookie's arm. "I don't think she did it either. I want to help her."

Tears welled in Cookie's eyes. "Ain't nothin' can help her now." Her features crumpled, and she felt for a chair.

"I don't believe that." Merry moved closer and put an arm around the woman.

Cookie's shoulders heaved, and she raised her apron to conceal her face. Merry's own eyes stung from unshed tears and her throat ached, but she could not give way to sentiment. If she had any hope of helping Jerusha, she had to keep her emotions under control, and as Graham had suggested, find evidence. At long last, Cookie lifted her face and swiped at her eyes. Without a glance for Merry she stood and settled back into the rhythm of her work.

"How long had Mr. Benning and Mr. Fraser done business together?" Merry asked.

"Sixteen, seventeen years. Long as Master Raleigh been alive. They met while Missus was expecting."

"Do you know what sorts of business interests they have in common?"

"I don't know nothing 'bout business."

"Have they visited before?"

Cookie sniffed, sighed, and turned back to her dough. "Once a year usually. They sail up from Charles Towne on one of their ships and stay for a month or so."

"How long have they been doing that?"

"Oh, ten years, maybe."

"Has this visit been different than any others?"

"Don't know. I don't see much of the family 'cept for Mrs. Benning. I'd say she and Mrs. Fraser are polite, but they ain't never been great friends. You'd do better to ask Jerusha or Isaiah."

"I'll do that." Merry pushed away from the table and stood. "Cookie, I will do everything I can to make sure justice prevails."

The old woman nodded, but didn't meet Merry's eyes.

With the children's breakfast tray balanced on her hip, Merry padded down the hall. Through the door of the morning room she heard the sound of the young master's voice raised against the softer timbre of what could only be his mother's voice. Merry paused, glancing to make sure she was alone in the corridor.

"I care not. I am nearly a man."

Merry could not make out Abigail's reply. She stepped closer to the door, taking care not to rattle the crockery.

"…what your father wanted, Raleigh."

"Then it is small wonder I am glad he is dead!" The pounding of boots warned Merry, and she scooted down the hall before it was flung open by the red-faced, tearful young man. He rushed past her, hardly seeming to notice her presence.

In the vacuum of his anger she could hear his mother weeping.

Merry bit her lip, the desire to comfort Abigail at war with the knowledge that she should not intrude. Abigail Benning had been a gentle and generous mistress, but that did not make them friends. It was no good thinking of what might have been if the circumstances had been different. Merry was a convict, and she'd do well not to forget it. At least, not until she could put her pardon to use.

She headed up the stairs and was about to enter the nursery when Mrs. Fraser's woman sidled into the hall, closing the door behind her as if it were made of porcelain.

Merry hoisted her tray higher and nodded a greeting. "Good morning. You're Nellie, aren't you?"

The woman raised her gaze from the ground as if startled to be addressed. "Mornin'."

She was a handsome woman with tawny skin, but some weight seemed to pull at her, grinding her shoulders down into a stoop.

Merry cast about for a means of prolonging the encounter. "Do you know where everything is? Do you need anything?"

The other woman paused. "I'm fine." She spoke quietly, almost furtively, as if unused to being addressed.

"You must have been here before."

She nodded. "The family has been coming here for years, and I've come with 'em ever since Mrs. Fraser made me her woman."

"Do you enjoy the visits?"

"It's a nice place. 'Course this time hasn't been the same, what with poor Mr. Benning being killed."

Nellie glanced side to side as if worried about eavesdroppers. "I feel real bad for poor Master Raleigh. Mrs. Fraser heard him having a big fight with his daddy right before he took sick. He's a good boy, but that kind of guilt can eat a boy up. Don't do nobody any good."

"Do the Frasers ever bring their children?"

"Don't have none. I best be getting Mrs. Fraser's morning tea. She don't like to be kept waiting."

"Of course. It was nice to meet you."

Merry shifted the breakfast tray again and entered the nursery. Something Nellie had said niggled at her, but she could not bring the thought into full bloom.

The children stirred as she entered, and she set the tray down gingerly.

She must find time to speak to Isaiah. He could tell her about Mr. Benning's business dealings. He might even be willing to tell her if there was bad blood between Mr. Benning and Mr. Fraser, provided she could find the right leverage.

Graham rubbed a damp palm on his breeches as he approached the Benning home. He'd grappled with the decision all night, just as Jacob had grappled with God. Merry might never speak to him after this, but he had to see her safe.

He half expected to be turned away as the house was in mourning, but Mrs. Benning agreed to see him, and he was shown into the drawing room.

He bowed over her hand and took the proffered seat.

"I understand that you have been bereaved, Mrs. Benning. I offer my sincerest condolences. I assure you I would not have intruded were it not important."

She was gracious, but grief seemed to have worn her thin as a tissue-paper doll. "Thank you, Mr. Sinclair. Isaiah said you have some news for me?"

"Yes madam. It's in regards to Miss Merry Lattimore. I believe she is indentured to this household?"

"Yes." A wary light glinted in her eyes. "I'm afraid she is

not for sale. Mr. Cleaves has been most persistent, but I cannot—will not—part with her."

Graham held up a hand. "No madam, that is not my intent. I've come from London." He explained his part in Merry's conviction and the subsequent discovery of Paget's guilt.

Almost in spite of herself, she seemed drawn into the tale. She nodded as he explained the circumstances of Paget's capture.

"Then she was not guilty at all."

"She was not. You can imagine my feelings at this discovery."

She nodded, as intent on the story as a small child.

"I have obtained a pardon from the king on her behalf. She is a free woman."

"We must tell her." Mrs. Benning nodded to a young slave boy standing at unobtrusive attention in the corner, and he scurried from the room.

In a few moments, Merry entered the drawing room. She looked much as usual until she saw him seated near Mrs. Benning. The color drained from her face in a rush, and she stumbled slightly.

Abigail Benning rushed to her side. "Oh my dear. I ought to have warned you. I know you do not associate this gentleman with entirely pleasant memories, but I assure you, he has rendered you a great service. Come. Come and sit with us."

Merry pulled back, shaking her head. "Ma'am, I could not."

"Nonsense. Oh, I have muddled this. Perhaps you ought to explain matters, Mr. Sinclair."

Graham stood until both Merry and Mrs. Benning had seated themselves.

Merry's lips were tipped up in a stiff smile, but her glare ate like acid.

He swallowed. "It's a long tale, but the essence is that

your innocence is known, and I have obtained a full pardon on your behalf."

Her jaw clenched so tightly he could nearly hear the grinding of her teeth. He cleared his throat. He had known she would be furious. Even so a sense of loss swept through him, and he realized how much he desired to reclaim her regard. And how unlikely it was.

Perhaps one day she would find it within her to forgive him. For everything. He squared his shoulders. If not, at least he would have the comfort of knowing that he had done what he could for her.

Heedless of the tension between them, Mrs. Benning embraced Merry. "Oh my dear, I am so happy for you. It is all so wonderful. You will stay with us of course, won't you? As my guest? I could not bear to lose you just now. And the children…"

Merry blinked and then smiled broadly. Her eyes glittered with triumph as she gazed at him over Mrs. Benning's shoulder. "Of course, I shall stay with you as long as you wish. I could never leave at such a time."

He gritted his teeth. *Blast it all anyway!* He ought to hire a berth on the next outbound ship, no matter its destination, simply to be away from her. Did she not see that her mission could be dangerous? He knew something of investigation, and it was not for the faint of heart.

Not that Merry was in any way faint of heart.

He stifled a sigh. He would simply have to talk some sense into her. In the meantime, he had promised to take on the slave woman's cause.

Heaven help him when he confessed to Connor.

"Mr. Sinclair, won't you stay and have some refreshments?" Mrs. Benning's features were animated now, and her smile seemed genuine.

He winced. "You are most kind, Mrs. Benning. But I don't

wish to tax your strength. Nor could I enjoy your hospitality under false pretenses."

Her smile melted into confusion.

He fumbled for words. "I have been asked to defend your slave woman against the charge of murder."

"What?"

"Do you believe her guilty?"

The color in her cheeks went the way of her smile. "I have known Jerusha all my life. She could never have done this. No one— It had to have been an accident. Nothing else makes any sense."

"Mrs. Benning." The sonorous voice of the elderly butler brought conversation to a halt.

"Yes, Isaiah?"

"Mr. Cleaves is here to see you, ma'am."

She sighed then squared her shoulders. "Show him in."

Merry shifted in her seat, but Mrs. Benning placed a hand on her arm. "Stay with me, dear."

Cleaves marched into the drawing room with a jaunty stride that spoke of a man who expected to get his way. "Mrs. Benning, I'm sure sorry to hear of your fine husband's passing. It's a sad day for Virginia. A sad day."

"Thank you, Mr. Cleaves." She pointedly did not invite him to sit.

His eyes flickered from Mrs. Benning's face to Merry's beside her to Graham. And then jerked back to Merry.

"Did you need something else, Mr. Cleaves?" Mrs. Benning's voice was frigidly polite.

"I just— That is…" His Adam's apple bobbed reflexively. "I've heard tattle about this young woman here. I thought, what with your husband's death and all, that you shouldn't be burdened with a rebellious and forward servant." Mrs. Benning's chilly stare seemed finally to penetrate his understanding, and his final words trailed off uncertainly. "I came to offer for her… ."

"Yes, well. I note your concern, but you need not fret on my account. Good day."

Befuddled, Cleaves clapped his hat back on his head. "Good day."

"And Mr. Cleaves. Please do not return in regards to this matter. Miss Lattimore's innocence has been acknowledged, and she has been pardoned. While she remains in Williamsburg, she will be my guest."

His nod was a single short jerk of his chin. "Good day." His stride was clipped and precise as he departed.

"Thank you." Merry reached for Mrs. Benning's hand.

"Think nothing of it, my dear. I am more than glad to see the back of that man." She smiled and touched the edge of Merry's apron. "We must see to making you look like a lady."

Graham smiled secretly. Abigail Benning was stronger than he would have credited. He would be leaving Merry in good hands.

Mrs. Benning turned to him. "Mr. Sinclair, I will be most grateful if you will defend Jerusha. Find out what really happened so that my husband may rest in peace."

Merry was sucked into a tempest of gowns and ribbons, frills and furbelows the moment Graham departed. Two maids worked on her hair while Abigail regarded her critically. They made a wall of skirts around her, hemming her in before the vanity.

With the backs of her fingers, Merry caressed the silk dressing gown she wore, taking care not to catch the fine thread with her work-roughened hands. It had been years since she had worn anything so fine. Merry recognized the impulse driving Abigail. In the wake of her father's death,

Merry had taken on any number of new projects. Anything to find distraction from her loss.

It was an altogether different prospect to be on the other end of such attention.

At least she'd had the satisfaction of seeing the look on Graham's face when she had been invited to stay in the house. It nearly made up for his conniving. Why had he suddenly assumed responsibility for her well-being? Where had he been for the last five years, when she could have used a friend? She shook off the frisson of resentment.

For now, the most important thing was that she could continue to try to discover who had really murdered Mr. Benning.

Would the slaves speak to her now? It would look odd if she continued to haunt the slave hall.

Hattie pulled her hair and she grimaced.

"Sorry, miss."

Merry raised a hand. There it was. The formality—the distance. It may already be too late to get any information from the staff.

On the other hand, her new status gave her greater license with the family and guests. She could ask questions of them now that might have gotten her punished for impertinence as a servant.

"Thank you for your kindness, Mrs. Benning. I am most grateful to you, especially at such a time."

"I am only sorry you've had to suffer so in the first place. I feel as if I've contributed to the injustice by buying your indenture." Abigail patted her shoulder.

"Oh no. You saved me. If Cleaves—" She shuddered. "I just wish there were something I could do to repay your kindness. I would remove your burden if I could."

Tears lurked in Abigail's eyes. "Thank you, but grief can only be healed by time."

"At least Master Raleigh is home. That must be a comfort."

"Poor Raleigh. He is so like his father." She reached forward and plucked a curl from its confines and placed it at Merry's temple. "I am not sure Charles Towne was altogether good for him. He seems not himself since he returned."

"Perhaps it is a symptom of grief, or simply a process of maturing?"

"Perhaps. Hopefully he will settle once classes resume at the college. He did very well last year. But his father wanted him to go to England and study law."

"He does not care for law?"

"He does not care for England."

Merry blinked, unsure whether she ought to be affronted on behalf of her homeland.

"He fell in with a group of agitators while at school. They are sowing discord all up and down the coast. They seem to set out each day looking for offence. Though from what I understand there have been some legitimate grievances. I do not follow politics, but I fear there is trouble brewing in these colonies."

"Was his father sending him to England to tear him away from unsuitable friends?"

"Oh no, I don't think so. He simply felt that law would be the best field for Raleigh."

"Mr. Sinclair passed the bar at the Middle Temple. I'm certain he has fond memories of his time there. Perhaps he could be prevailed upon to speak to Master Raleigh. That is, if you intend to encourage him to follow his father's wishes."

"That may be just the thing Raleigh needs. He is so headstrong at times."

Abigail pinned a final ribbon in the back of Merry's hair then patted her shoulder. "You look lovely."

For the first time since being plunked down in front of the glass, Merry focused on her image. Her hair was piled high, though mercifully not powdered. Between that and her fine gown, she bore little resemblance to the bedraggled woman who arrived in Virginia aboard a convict hulk.

She raised a tentative hand to her cheek. "I hardly know myself."

"Oh my dear. Fate has played on you so unfairly. It is time that something good should happen." A playful smile crossed Abigail's features. "Now you must tell me about Mr. Sinclair. I think there must be more to the story than I have been privy to."

The click of heeled shoes stopped by the open door. "The funeral must be starting now." Mrs. Fraser's observation brought instant tears to Abigail's eyes.

Merry shot the woman a hard glare. Could she not let Abigail forget about her loss even for a few moments? No, she must dredge it all back up and then top it with a dose of guilt.

"I wish I could be there with Raleigh. He's young to bear such a burden." Abigail looked down, her fingers plucking at invisible bits of lint on Merry's shoulder. "And I would have liked one more chance to bid Reginald farewell. I don't know how we shall all get on without him."

"That would hardly be fitting. You do best by staying decently with your children and allowing the gentlemen to attend to such ghoulish duties. My husband will take great pains to ensure that Raleigh is comforted." Catherine Fraser's brisk tone held no understanding.

Abigail straightened as if she'd been doused with a bucket of rainwater. "We are lucky you have been with us at this time."

Merry watched Abigail closely. If there was any irony in the comment it was so well hidden as to be indiscernible.

They repaired to the parlor for a genteel tea, and as the ladies talked over their memories of Mr. Benning, Merry's mind wandered to her earlier conversation with Abigail. She had been given much to consider.

If Master Raleigh had fallen in with a crowd of political troublemakers, was it possible his newfound convictions were so strongly held that he would do anything to avoid consorting with the enemy?

Graham inhaled and wished he hadn't. The prison's stench was thick with the pungent musk of despair. His eyes adjusted slowly from the brightness of the Virginian sun.

"Jerusha?"

He heard a scrabble in the corner and finally saw her, hunched in so deeply on herself that he had missed her presence.

"Yes sir." Her voice rasped as if she had been coughing, or perhaps crying, a great deal.

"My name is Graham Sinclair."

"Yes sir. I know you."

"I have obtained permission to speak in the yard. Would you care to step outside?"

The prisoners' yard was a pitiful little brick-and-stone courtyard perhaps ten feet wide and fifteen feet long. Its only advantage was that it allowed them to speak away from the ears of the other prisoners.

She squinted in the light, and her reddened eyes bore witness that his surmise of recent weeping had been correct.

"Miss Lattimore has been busy on your behalf."

The comment coaxed an almost-smile from the woman. "She's a loyal girl, and kind."

"But perhaps a bit naive?" Graham completed the sentiment she could not seem to bring herself to voice.

Jerusha shrugged.

"I'm a lawyer. She has requested that I take on the defense of your case."

She looked up at him sharply. "Is that allowed?"

"There is no law preventing it."

She looked at him askance, as if realizing he had not exactly answered her question.

"Do you know anything about this murder?"

She shook her head adamantly. "I don't know nothing about it."

He eyed her steadily. "Jerusha, you know the household, you know the people. Servants hear a great deal of the most intimate discourse. You are privy to more about your mistress than even most of her family. You must have heard or seen something."

"No sir. I don't take account of nothing that ain't my business."

Graham restrained a sigh. She had to say it of course; she could not admit to hearing the conversations that whirled about her. Slaves had been flogged to death for repeating gossip about their masters. But the keeper would be back in a few moments to send him about his business.

"Jerusha, I don't have much time. You must tell me if you saw or heard anything suspicious."

"Mr. Sinclair, sir, I learned long ago it don't do to speak ill of white folk. I don't know no reason anybody'd want to kill Master."

Time to try a different tack. "Had he been acting differently of late?"

"Not that I recall. He was just himself. Except…"

He latched onto it. "Except what?"

She glanced around again and lowered her voice. "He seemed worried. He and Mister Fraser were at odds. Don't ask me. I don't know why. I take care of Miz Benning, and the gentlemen didn't say anything quarrelsome in front of the ladies. They just weren't as friendly-like as they used to be. And then there—" Once more she skidded to a stop, midsentence.

He took her arm, perhaps a bit more roughly than he intended since she winced. She did not pull away though, accepting the pain as if it were to be expected. He loosened his grip.

A key scraped in the courtyard's gate.

"You must tell me whatever you know."

"Mr. Benning's been upset with Master Raleigh. It was silly, an argument, no more. They would have made up in a few days, and things would have gone back to normal."

The keeper appeared, blowing his nose into a large, grayish handkerchief. "Time's up."

Jerusha reached a hand toward him and then snatched it back. "Is my Abigail well?"

Graham nodded. "She is holding up, though I think the loss has wounded her deeply."

Tears pooled in her eyes and spilled over onto her cheeks. "I didn't kill 'im. Please tell her."

The turnkey cleared his throat pointedly.

"She doesn't think you did." He would have liked to offer some sort of comfort, but could think of no hope to extend her.

Merry swept into the dining room on Raleigh Benning's arm. As she took her seat, she peeked up at him through demure lashes. Though only seventeen, he had his father's elegant leanness and stood half a head taller than she. His eyes came straight from his mother however. Now they were stormy, though he troubled to offer her a smile.

They were a small party, just the household and Mr. Sinclair. It would not be fitting to entertain at such a time. Still, Merry's fingers returned again and again to caressing the lush brocade of her skirts, and her nose quivered at the tantalizing smells of roasted meat, fine sauces, and freshly baked bread. Smells she had sought to ignore for months so as not to be driven mad with longing.

Despite the witness of the looking glass, Merry could not quite reconcile herself to the notion that she was no longer a servant. She felt at once both small and grubby, and overlarge and clumsy. A spectacle, that's what she was. The only saving grace was that there were not many spectators.

Mr. Fraser's eyes raked her from stem to stern. "My wife told me of your good fortune, Merry." He welcomed her as if he were the host rather than a guest himself. "I'm sure we are all pleased at your extraordinary luck."

Merry's cheeks tingled, and she withdrew her hand from his grip. To still use her given name, so informally. He acted as if she were not innocent all along, but had simply wriggled through some fantastical loophole.

"Thank you, Mr. Fraser." She managed to incline her head with a measure of dignity. She at least knew how to conduct herself.

Graham leaned forward across the table slightly. "Miss Lattimore"—was it just Merry or had he stressed the appropriate form of address?—"has been through a great ordeal. I for one am most relieved that her reputation has been fully restored."

Mr. Fraser pursed his lips, and the line of his jaw tightened. An instant later the expression disappeared into a toothy grin. "Hear, hear." Mr. Fraser raised his glass. "To Miss Lattimore."

The others had no choice but to follow suit, though it hardly seemed in the best taste to be toasting at dinner when Mr. Benning had been buried that afternoon.

"I imagine you will be returning to England now that you are at liberty?" Mrs. Fraser's smile looked as thin as Merry's felt.

Mr. Fraser flourished his knife, spattering the table with sauce from his squab. "I believe the sloop in port at Yorktown will be sailing within the week."

Despite his apparent goodwill, Merry could not find it within herself to like the gentleman. She watched with dis-

taste as he shoveled another bite into his maw, no more man-
nered than one of the convicts with whom she had been caged.

"It has all happened so quickly that I hardly know what to
do. Indeed, I do not even know what my options are."

"Surely you do not mean to say that you would consider
staying here?" Mrs. Fraser dabbed at the corners of her mouth
with her napkin.

Abigail looked up from her plate. "Oh, I wish you would."

The houseboys presented the next course with the unobtrusive precision of a well-executed minuet.

Merry smiled at her. "I would not leave you at such a time
in any event. There is time enough for me to return to England."

"Then we shall have the pleasure of your company for a
while longer." Mr. Fraser lifted his glass, and for a moment
Merry feared he would propose another toast. He merely
drank deeply and followed with a too-large bite of roasted
beef.

"Mr. Sinclair, do you have any notion how long your ob-
ligations will keep you here?" Merry was desperate enough
to turn the conversation away from herself that she had no
compunction in throwing Graham to the wolves.

"Williamsburg will miss the presence of such a polished,
handsome gentleman." Mrs. Fraser sounded as distressed at
the notion of Graham leaving as she had at the thought that
Merry might be staying.

He cleared his throat. "I am not certain my business will
be so neatly concluded. Matters of law can often be compli-
cated by unforeseen circumstances."

"A lawyer, eh?" Mr. Fraser held his glass up for Daniel
to refill.

Graham inclined his head. "A barrister. Although I have
not practiced in a good while. I am compelled by circumstance to return to my old occupation."

Mr. Fraser's eyebrows lifted in exaggerated inquiry. "I took you for a solicitor. I suppose it must be a personal matter, if you would prolong your stay here. Perhaps you are considering establishing a business in Williamsburg. We are flourishing."

A calculating gleam entered Graham's eye, and his chin tilted, oh so slightly. Merry had seen that look on any number of occasions, from considering a horse for purchase, to crafting a strategy to confound one of his professors. It generally preceded something outrageous.

"Actually, sir, I have committed to defend the slave woman, Jerusha, against the charge of murder."

Mrs. Fraser spluttered and coughed into her glass. Graham turned to her, offering his napkin. Her husband paid no mind. He half stood. "You presume on Mrs. Benning's kindness! I will ask you to leave, sir."

At Merry's side, Raleigh Benning also rose. "Mr. Fraser, this is not your household that you can—"

Abigail raised a hand in a gesture as peremptory as a general's signal. "Mr. Fraser, you will not speak to a guest at my table in such a manner." Her voice brooked no quibbling. "Raleigh, Mr. Fraser is also our guest. Now, I assure you both that I wholly support Mr. Sinclair's efforts. I do not for a moment believe Jerusha killed my husband. There has been some mistake."

Mr. Fraser resumed his seat, his mumbled apology less than convincing. Brow furrowed, he stared at his plate as if he had forgotten what he had been in the midst of doing.

Mrs. Fraser had overcome her coughing fit, though her voice sounded strained. "But slaves are well known for their scheming. It wouldn't be the first time one poisoned their master. The penchant is well documented."

Merry sought Daniel. He stood by the sideboard, his eyes

staring into nothingness. Did she not realize that Jerusha's son was at hand?

Raleigh spoke for the first time. "Not Jerusha." Scarlet spots seared his cheekbones in asymmetrical splotches. His glare dared anyone to argue with him.

Head held high, Abigail stretched her lips into a smile. "I do appreciate your concern for our family, Mr. Fraser. Perhaps we could turn the conversation to less painful topics? Mr. Sinclair, we are most pleased to have your company for as long as possible."

Graham inclined his head. "Thank you, madam."

Merry regarded Abigail as she shepherded the conversation through the next course. A formidable spirit lived within her delicate frame. She had to look closely to notice that the skin around Abigail's eyes was pulled taut with strain, and her mouth was ringed with a tense white line. Her eyes were dry, but reddened, and she blinked often. She ought to rest, but seemed unable to accord herself the luxury.

Merry turned her attention to her plate. She had not eaten so well in many months. Despite dreaming of such a moment, she found she was ill equipped to stomach the bounty. Indeed, she was growing queasy. She pushed the remaining food around, like a child hoping that a detested vegetable will disappear if prodded enough.

Her flagging attention was brought back to the conversation by Mr. Fraser's raised voice.

"I wonder at your obstinacy, young sir." Mr. Fraser tossed his napkin on the table.

Raleigh Benning regarded the older gentleman from beneath lowering brows. The smoldering rage in his eyes sent a chill up Merry's spine. Such bitterness...

"I shall thank you not to presume too much upon our acquaintance, sir. You are not my father."

Fraser's eyes widened and his nostrils flared. "You should

be glad of that, my boy. If a child of mine treated a friend of the family, who only sought his good, with such impertinence I should have him horsewhipped."

"I shall count my blessings then." Raleigh shoved away from the table. "Mother, ladies, I bid you good evening." He offered a perfunctory bow before marching from the room.

"You will have to take that boy in hand." Mr. Fraser was not yet done putting a damper on the meal. "He will require a stepfather to keep him in line. I understand that he ran with a most unpleasant crowd while at William and Mary. We kept him from such things while in Charles Towne of course. But now that he has been returned, he will need watching. A devotee of Patrick Henry, of all people. Those fellows are all rabble-rousers. Mark my words." He stabbed the table with a forefinger. "You will need to marry again soon. It will require a man's strength of will to keep that lad in check."

Abigail sat so still that she might have been carved of alabaster. Only her eyes snapped with fiery outrage. Even Mr. Fraser must have sensed that he had gone too far. Uncomfortable silence settled over the table.

"Mr. Fraser." Abigail's voice held an edge like sharpened iron. "I shall be most grateful if you would refrain from such comments. My husband was only buried this morning. I do not care to be married off again so soon, nor do I wish my son upset further with talk of being sent away. I am sure you understand."

Merry was sure of no such thing.

Clearing his throat, Fraser wiped his mouth with the napkin he had tossed aside earlier. "Apologies. Meant no offense. I'm merely advising you as I know Reginald would have wished me to."

"I appreciate your concern, and I will call upon you as I have need." As regal as any duchess, Abigail stood. "Ladies, perhaps it is time we withdraw and allow the gentlemen to enjoy some port."

More than happy to leave the table, Merry stood and hurried to the door then stepped aside to allow Mrs. Benning and Mrs. Fraser to precede her. She glanced back hoping to catch Graham's eye. Instead, she found Mr. Fraser staring at her with a narrowed, calculating gaze.

Chapter 8

"Mr. Sinclair." Merry pulled her wrap more tightly around her shoulders. She glanced furtively around. "Mr. Sinclair," she hissed again.

He stopped and turned to her, retracing his steps along the oyster-shell path. "If we are going to continue these midnight assignations, you may as well call me Graham."

"This is no assignation."

"What do you call it, pray tell?"

"I…" Merry sucked in a calming breath. "Have you matured at all since nineteen?"

He flashed a grin. "Some."

"I fail to see it." She waved an impatient hand. "There is little time for games. I wanted to share what I have discovered."

"Yes, that dinner was perhaps the least successful I have ever attended." He drew closer. "And yet it provided a most interesting glimpse into the relationships of these characters."

"They are not characters. They are people."

"Poor Miss Lattimore, has life used you so cruelly that you have abandoned all the joy and whimsy I always associated with you?"

Her cheeks flamed in irritation, and it was an effort to keep her voice lowered. "Yes, they have abandoned me. Now, will you please listen?"

At last chastened, he nodded. "Let us step away from the house at least."

Hand on her elbow he steered her beneath a graceful old oak. They stood close together in the gloom of the overarching branches, curiously intimate in their seclusion from the rest of the world.

Merry's breath seemed overly loud all of a sudden. The heat radiating from Graham's body seeped into her, and she relinquished her grip on her wrap. She closed her eyes briefly. What would it be like to relinquish control of herself as well? To just be held? To let him stroke her hair and tell her it would all be well?

"Well?"

Merry blinked. Now it was she distracted by foolishness. "I apologize, I'm woolgathering."

"Is it possible that Raleigh Benning killed his father?"

She shook her head. "Don't be daft."

"Did you not hear the passion in him? The notion of going to London fills him with dread."

"I'll grant you that he does not care for the idea, but I cannot credit he would deliberately kill his father."

"Perhaps in the heat of an argument he lost his head and lashed out in desperation."

"If Mr. Benning had been killed by a blow to the head I might be able to credit your theory, but he was poisoned. That requires deliberation."

"He does not seem much affected by the death."

If only she could see Graham's face she could read his intentions better. Was he playing devil's advocate, or did he really think Raleigh Benning might have murdered his father? "I think he is more grieved than he appears. He masks his pain in anger."

"His grief could contain a large measure of remorse."

"I am convinced of it, but not because he killed his father, merely because they argued before he died."

He cocked his head to the side. "Aren't you taking a great deal on trust?"

"Perhaps you have never felt such a degree of fury. I have. I know what it is like to be angry enough to kill, and yet not to strike out. I learned it was possible just before I left London."

His voice softened. "Merry—"

She held up a hand to ward off the words, though he probably couldn't see it. "Can you look into Mr. Fraser's business relationship with Mr. Benning? He is my choice of suspect. I have been unable to learn a thing about their dealings. It's not the sort of matter they discussed with their slaves. Though the servants know about almost everything else."

"I already have Connor looking into things. But do not close your mind to other possibilities." He leaned a shoulder against the oak. "Have you considered Mrs. Benning?"

"Abigail? Why?"

"A great number of murders are committed by the spouses of the victim. And I saw a formidable strength of will in her."

Merry shook her head. "Absolutely not. Abigail had nothing to do with his death. I would swear to it."

"How can you be so certain?"

"I know her. She is not capable of murder. Certainly not that of her husband. They were in love."

"We must at least consider her. If you truly want to see Jerusha freed, we must consider someone."

"I tell you she did not do it." She dropped her voice to a

feathery hiss. "I realize that people are capable of the foulest deeds, but Abigail Benning had no reason to kill her husband. She loved him more now than when they first married."

He cleared his throat. "What if he had...betrayed that love?"

"The slaves would know."

"Do not be blind to the possibility." Stiffening, he peeled himself away from the tree and gripped her arms. "You must be on guard at all times. If you were to slip and let someone know that you are trying to discover the murderer, you could be in grave danger." He shifted even closer and raised a hand to cup her cheek.

She longed to see his face better, to read the message his eyes contained. Her heart pounded, sending the blood rushing pell-mell through her veins and scattering her thoughts.

She had craved this since leaving England. A comforting arm. Someone to rely on other than herself. How nice it would be to simply turn over all responsibility and allow Graham to handle matters.

A flutter of panic plucked at her chest. She would never again make the mistake of blindly trusting that matters would work out simply because it was just. If things were going to be set right for Jerusha, it would be because Merry made certain it happened. Graham might do what he could, but he might just as easily change his mind. After all, he'd left her when she needed him.

The delicateness of Merry's cheekbone cradled in the palm of Graham's hand made his heart constrict. Had she eaten anything since leaving England?

She seemed to lean into him, and he inhaled the lilac scent of her hair. She was no longer the girlish miss of his memory, but fully a woman. A groan stuck in his throat as he fought the instinct to draw her closer, crush her to his chest, to feel the press of her body against his.

What would she do if he lowered his mouth over hers? He blinked.

She stiffened, straightened, pulled away. Perhaps she could discern his thoughts.

He cleared his throat of confusion. "I promise to do all I can for your Jerusha. But you must promise to be cautious. I cannot bear the notion of you being in danger again."

His arms hung at his sides, empty.

"I need to get back to the house." Her voice held a wistful note.

Mayhap she did not want to leave?

What was he thinking? He had condemned this woman to horrors he couldn't imagine. It was scarcely a recipe for courtship.

She slipped away from him as quiet as a wraith in the darkness. "Thank you. I know this is not what you intended when you left England. I hope you are able to return as soon as you wished." She whirled, lifted her skirts, and darted for the house.

Graham sighed. It was entirely possible he had taken on more than he could handle with this case. He rubbed a hand over the stubble forming on his chin and turned toward his lodgings.

Upon entering, he found that Connor had waited up for him.

"Learn anything?" Graham sat on his bed with enough force that the ticking on either end went airborne, as if the feathers had not forgotten how to fly.

"A bit."

"Spill it, Connor. I'm exhausted." Graham pulled off a boot and allowed it to thud to the floor.

"There isn't much to spill. Fraser and Benning were partners in several ventures. They jointly owned three different ships transporting cotton, rice, indigo, and tobacco from the colonies to England and returning with tea, woolens, and the trappings of civilization."

"What else?"

"An auction house and a silver smithy. Their plantations are separately held, and each has other sole holdings."

"Any hint of shady dealings?"

"Not a whisper, but I'm just getting started. If there are any grubs under the rocks, I'll dig 'em up."

"We may have to begin looking at the son."

"He's young, isn't he? Just a lad?"

"Seventeen or so. Seems he's cast his lot in with the rabble-rousers who have been putting His Majesty's nose out of joint."

"Seems a leap from there to murdering his own father."

Graham worked at his other boot. "His father wanted him to go to the Middle Temple to study law. Zealotry is a strange creature. It can blind an otherwise reasonable person to his own folly. He finds all manner of justification for his behavior."

"But this is a poisoning. Lads strike out in anger. They don't usually have the foresight to employ poison."

"Poison is a woman's weapon?" Graham paused and glanced up.

Connor shrugged. "Did you consider the wife?"

"I tried." Graham immediately regretted the acerbity of his tone. "Merry is decidedly opposed to the notion that it is even possible."

"*Merry* is it?"

"Not to you." Graham let his other boot fall, though he would have preferred to heave it at Connor's smug smile. "She will not dictate whom we can investigate. I intend to save Jerusha's life, but I very much fear it may be a Pyrrhic victory."

* * *

Afternoon sun streamed through the drawing room windows, setting the dust motes aglitter. Merry watched as they swirled and glided in unending dance. The need to yawn niggled at the back of her throat, and she inhaled through her nose as deeply as she could, trying to forestall the inevitable.

She plunged her needle back through the fine muslin secured in her hoop and formed another tiny stitch. Out on the lawn she heard John's throaty giggle and smiled. Despite the blow of their father's passing, the children were fully recovered from their illness.

A bit of iron from her busk poked her in the side and she shifted.

Mrs. Fraser's too-refined voice carried on in seeming perpetual soliloquy. "The royal governor wrote personally to thank me for my support. He said that without such support as mine, the museum never would have been founded. It's the first in the colonies, you know. I feel quite humbled to know I had a hand in it. I always say it is important to be civically minded. Our countrymen can learn a good deal by studying culture. It will raise the moral tone. Of course, I quite understand that Williamsburg is a smallish place. It would be difficult to organize something so ambitious here—"

"Oh, I don't know," Abigail broke in, a smile crinkling the fine skin around her eyes. "We have managed to complete the Public Hospital. I'm told it will open any day."

"Yes, well, a hospital such as that is scarcely a bastion of culture and good taste." Mrs. Fraser set aside her sewing and reached for her snuffbox.

"Too true, but it does speak to the compassion of our House of Burgesses, and it will provide a valuable benefit to our citizens."

Mrs. Fraser took a delicate pinch of snuff. "My dear Abigail, it is to house mental incompetents. Not really the sort of place one would want one's name associated with. Now, if you turned your attention to patronizing the arts—"

"Oh dear," said Abigail.

"Is something the matter?" Mrs. Fraser dabbed at her nose with a filmy white handkerchief.

"I seem to have run out of black ribband."

Merry shifted her aching shoulders. "I would be pleased to run to the milliner's."

Abigail looked up from her handiwork. "Would you?"

"Of course."

"Well, if you do not mind. There are one or two other trifles I could use. Have them put on our account." Abigail busied herself with writing out a list of the required items.

Merry neatly folded up her sewing and put it away.

With a conspiratorial wink, Abigail handed her the list. "It is a beautiful afternoon, my dear. Take your time."

A corresponding smile burst from Merry as she understood. Poor Abigail, she could not save herself from another tedious afternoon with Mrs. Fraser, but she could fall on her sword and give Merry leave to save herself.

Abigail waved her away. "And do take one of the slaves to carry things."

Merry inclined her head. "Yes ma'am." She had just the person in mind.

She found Isaiah in the butler's pantry polishing the silver. "I'm going to the milliner's to fetch some things for Mrs. Benning. Would you come with me?"

"Yes ma'am." He wiped his hands on the apron he wore to protect his clothing and slipped it over his head. "You want me to fetch the cart?"

Merry blinked. She hadn't been offered the use of a carriage for her convenience in…ever. The offer sounded ludicrous in its luxury. But they would have more time to converse if they were on foot. Regretfully she declined the offer.

Isaiah retrieved a large basket, and they set out.

"How long did you serve Mr. Benning?"

"Oh, I was his man since we was just striplings."

"It must be strange to think he is gone."

"That it is, miss. I never thought I'd see the day... ." He shook his head.

"Do you believe Jerusha poisoned him?"

He hesitated. "That's what they's sayin'."

Merry cocked her head, looking up at him sideways. "I don't believe a word of it. Jerusha would no more harm the Bennings than you. Mrs. Benning agrees."

His mouth sagged open a touch, and his eyebrows pulled together. "Mrs. Benning said that?"

Merry nodded.

"I surely am glad to hear it." His dark eyes bored into her. "Do you think there's hope for Jerusha?"

Merry paused. She didn't want to provide false expectation, but neither did she wish to dash the tentative hope she saw in his eyes. "Our belief in her innocence means little. We must find the means to prove it."

"How you goin' to do that?"

"What can you tell me of Mr. Benning's business dealings? Particularly as they relate to Mr. Fraser?"

"I don't know as there's much I *can* tell. Mr. Benning's clerk, Mr. Porter, would know all 'bout that—"

A commotion down the street snatched at Merry's attention, and she turned her head.

It couldn't be. What was he doing now?

Graham grabbed for his hat as it tumbled from his head. He whirled to face the culprit. "Apologize, sir!"

Mr. Cleaves crossed his arms. His nose turned up in a caricature of disgust. "It only stands to reason that a man who would choose to advocate for a Negress should be undressed in public."

Three ruffians, either sons or apprentices, closed in hard by the man's shoulder.

Graham narrowed his eyes. "Have you a quarrel with me, sir?" He felt Connor taking up position at his own shoulder.

"Why? Do you intend to call me out?"

"Perhaps. Do you intend to continue being an insufferable lout?"

Cleaves flushed, his arms dropped to his sides, and he stepped closer. "We don't need the likes of you coming to Virginia and stirring up trouble among the slaves."

The louder Cleaves became, the more passersby stopped to watch.

Graham looked down the end of his nose at the tradesman. "Treating your slaves with a modicum of decency will do more toward dampening unrest than rushing to judgment." He held up the tip of his walking stick while discreetly redistributing his weight and bending ever so slightly at the knee. "But I shall make allowances for your error. A mere bully boy cannot be expected to understand deeper considerations."

A hoot of laughter went up from the men surrounding the tavern door.

Cleaves rushed forward, his fist raised.

Graham braced for the attack. He was in no mood to be trifled with, and the jackanapes would get the beating he so clearly required.

"There you are!" A flurry of flowered, beribboned femininity inserted itself between Graham and the charging bull.

The latter stumbled to a stop.

Graham blinked and looked down to find Merry Lattimore dressed in the finest Williamsburg could offer and looking lovely. Her smile might well have been spread on with a trowel, however, for it did not reach her eyes, which snapped with fury.

"I have been looking everywhere." She looped her arm through his. "Good afternoon, gentlemen." She tossed a rosy smile over her shoulder in coquettish fashion then led him away, prattling on about an errand at the milliner's shop.

Graham glanced over his shoulder. Her manservant and Connor flanked them, while the befuddled tradesman still stood with his arm raised.

Graham's fingers clenched into fists. "What do you think you are doing?"

"I'd ask you the same," she hissed. "Brawling in the street like some urchin? Such behavior does not befit the dignity of a magistrate…or a barrister. And it will win you no friends among the gentlemen of this city."

She was right of course, but he itched to pound something, and Cleaves would have done nicely.

Raleigh Benning appeared at his side. "I saw that."

Graham glanced at him. "Yes?"

"That was Thomas Cleaves. Don't listen to a thing he says. He thinks that because he is rich he can do anything he wants."

"Oh yes?"

Raleigh nodded. "There are many of his type around the college. They beat their servants and families and think they are big men. I say they are small men with small minds. They know nothing of the principles of liberty."

Graham looked sidewise at the lad. "On that we are agreed."

Raleigh Benning offered him a cocky smirk. "Many nations suffer the same lack of understanding, I think."

Graham returned the smile and touched the brim of his hat, acknowledging the young man's score.

Raleigh nodded, and his expression softened into a genuine smile. "Had it come to open battle, I would have joined your side. Jerusha would never hurt my father, and that means someone else did. I would consider it a service to my family if you find the person responsible."

Graham halted to turn and look Raleigh in the eye. He placed a hand on the young man's shoulder. "I give you my solemn oath to do everything in my power."

"Thank you, sir." Moisture flooded Raleigh's eyes, and he cleared his throat. "I must be off." He tipped his tricorn. "Miss Lattimore, gentlemen."

He hastened down a side street leaving Graham to stare after him.

"If that lad killed his father, I'll eat my stockings," Connor said.

Graham turned to him. "Hardly evidence worthy of the court's consideration."

"Don't mean it's not worthy of ours."

"Miss Lattimore, may I present Connor Cray, the most contrary man in the world, and the best friend."

Merry dipped into a curtsey as she extended her hand to Connor. She was regaining the unconscious grace she had carried as a young girl. Perhaps there was hope that her experiences had not damaged her beyond repair.

"Mr. Cray, I am delighted to make your acquaintance."

"Oh, we met before, miss. Back in Mr. Sinclair's magistrate's office."

Her cheeks bloomed as red as a peony, and Graham caught a flash of white as she briefly caught at her lip with her teeth. But then she swallowed. "Then I am pleased to meet you again in better circumstances."

"And I you. Gra—Mr. Sinclair was as testy as an old goat until he obtained your pardon. He couldn't think of anything else."

Merry glanced up at Graham, and their gazes collided. "Indeed?"

Her coffee dark eyes held his.

"Yes ma'am. He couldn't sleep for weeks."

Graham cleared his throat. "May we escort you somewhere?"

"I am on my way to the milliner's." At last she broke her gaze.

Graham drooped. Ben Franklin's electrical experiments might be advanced exponentially if he could harness the power in Merry Lattimore's eyes.

Chapter 9

Merry turned her face away from the street and adjusted her veil. Her reputation had just been restored, no sense in inviting recognition. She rapped on the door to Sarah's fine house.

Her fingers tapped a restless tattoo against her skirt. She raised a fist to the door again. It swung in before she could strike, and she stepped forward involuntarily. She adjusted her veil again. "Is Mrs. Proctor home?"

"She's sleeping." The maid's bleary eyes and disheveled hair suggested that she had been doing the same.

Merry plastered on a cajoling smile. "I am sorry for disturbing you, but it is most urgent that I speak with her."

The maid sighed, but stepped back, allowing Merry just enough room to squeeze through into the house.

"I'll go ask if she will receive you."

Merry nodded. Fair enough. She toyed with the fringe on her reticule as she waited for the maid to return. Had Graham been as upset by her sentencing as Mr. Cray implied? Could it be that she had been as harsh as he in her judgment. Or perhaps even harsher. She swallowed hard against the notion.

"This way."

Merry jumped at the break in her reverie and followed the maid upstairs. She found Sarah still abed.

Her friend extended a languid hand, but retracted it to smother a yawn.

"What is it, Merry?"

"I'm afraid I have another favor to beg."

Sarah shifted her covers. "More money?"

"No. In fact, I've brought your coin back." Merry plopped the heavy purse onto the mattress.

"Then what?"

"The friend I told you of has been taken up for murder."

Sarah's eyes widened, and she put a hand to her mouth. "What happened?"

In terse sentences, Merry sketched out the details. She could not sit still, and found herself wearing a trough in Sarah's Wilton carpet.

Sarah shook her head. "It's terrible, but I don't see that your Jerusha has a hope."

"She did not do it."

"She is a Negress. Her trial will have even less to do with justice than mine would if I were accused of murder."

"I refuse to believe that justice can only be afforded to the well-to-do."

Sarah shook her head. "Don't be naive." Her tone was a lash, bringing blood stinging into Merry's cheeks. "Money is only one factor. I have coin enough, but in many respects I am as much a slave as Jerusha. I am bound by my occupation as surely as she is fettered by the color of her skin. Neither of us will ever be given the benefit of the doubt."

"If we provide evidence that someone else committed the crime, they will have to listen to reason."

Again, Sarah shook her head, her pretty lips turned up in a resigned half smile. "What do you wish of me?"

"The *Nyriad* is in port. It was owned by Mr. Benning and his partner. If any of the crew come to your house, would you endeavor to discover whether they have ever heard of any dubious dealings?"

"That ought to be easy enough."

"Be discreet."

"My dear, men say women are gossips, but once you get a man gabbing there is no stopping him."

"Thank you, Sarah."

"Think nothing of it, my girl." Sarah offered a genuine smile now, her pique evidently forgotten or at least forgiven. "Shall I send round a note if I learn anything?"

"Yes, that shouldn't be a problem now."

"Ah, then now we can discuss what interests me." Sarah plucked at the fine linen of Merry's skirts. "Where did you get these new togs? Not to mention the wherewithal to come a-visiting in the morning?"

Graham pushed away from the table and rubbed his eyes. He needed a drink. Law texts were so dry they sucked the moisture right out of a man. His lamp flickered, and he reached to the sideboard for his mug. Tepid lemon water would not have been his first choice, but he would make do. He quaffed the drink and smacked his lips at the tartness.

The piled books glared at him like a pack of disapproving dons. He ground his teeth. He left Oxford years ago, but it had never left him.

Kneading the back of his neck with one hand he flipped the page of the enormous text before him. Hmm. Perhaps if he appealed to the Virginians' notion of the principles of property ownership. He dipped his quill in the inkpot and began sketching out his defense.

Merry's image rose before his mind's eye. Her eyes had haunted him for months now. He would not fail her.

The knob rattled, and Connor stepped over the threshold.

Hungry for the distraction, Graham turned to him. "What news?"

"You owe me two quid."

Making a show of grousing, Graham dug in his pockets and counted out the sum in the smallest denominations he could find. "I hope I got my money's worth."

"I think you'll be pleased."

"Would you care to elaborate?"

Connor's rigid stoicism cracked, and a grin split his features. "I thought you'd never ask." He settled onto his bed and loosened his stock.

Graham smiled back and shook his head. "Out with it, man!"

"All right, no need to shout." The great lout stifled a chuckle and narrowly averted a bloody nose by beginning, "I couldn't turn up a hint of scandal 'bout Mrs. Benning. Seems a lady of blameless and upright habits. 'Course I ain't talked to her servants. Miss Lattimore chased me away 'fore I could strike up any interesting conversations. She told me she'd speak to you later."

That should be an enjoyable conversation. "Is that it?"

Connor slid him a sly sidewise glance. "Not by a long shot. There is a lad what works at the warehouse Mr. Benning owned. I loosened him up with a couple of pints of ale over at Chowning's Tavern, and when we were friendly, he tells me as how Mr. Fraser has taken over care of the books in the last two years. He also found as how there were two different insurances taken out on the same cargo. One here in Williamsburg in the firm's name, and one in only Fraser's name, taken out by a company down in Charles Towne.

"He would never have known, but for coming across a

copy of the policy once when Mr. Fraser was here last year. Seems this ship in question, the *Phoenix*, sank in a sudden gale. Apparently it was a real shame. She was fully laden, on a return trip from England, and went down within a couple leagues of the port in Charles Towne."

Graham straightened in his chair. He'd known there was something off about Fraser. Merry would be delighted. "How convenient."

"Wasn't it just."

"Did he have the policy, or can he get it?"

"Wouldn't clap to the notion, I'm afraid. Doesn't want to be out of a job."

"I suppose he'll not testify then."

"Nope. Looked like a vicar at a bull-baiting when I asked him about it ever so gentle-like."

Graham rested his chin on his knuckles. "It's a start. If there was this, there will be more." He glared at the wall before him as if the answers he sought might suddenly be written there.

They had a good deal of investigation yet to do. Preventing the exposure of a fraud might be enough to drive a man to murder, but who was to say Benning hadn't been in on the deal? Still, the second policy in only Fraser's name was suggestive. He needed to speak to Benning's clerk as soon as possible.

"Do you think—" His question was interrupted by a snore. Connor had changed clothes and gone to bed.

Graham blew out the lamp and stood, stretching.

It mightn't work, but at least he now had a strategy.

Merry closed her eyes and raised her face to the sun's caress. The rich smell of the soil and sun-warmed herbs seemed almost another personality working alongside her and Abigail.

"It is beastly out here. I don't know how you both can

stand it." Perched gingerly on a cushioned seat, Mrs. Fraser swatted at a bumblebee droning lazily near her ear. "Pay attention, you foolish girl."

Nellie started to attention and shifted the enormous parasol she held so that no bit of Mrs. Fraser's person should be exposed to the sunlight.

Pink faced and smudged, Abigail looked up from her weeding next to Merry. "But it is such a lovely day, Catherine. Just smell the flowers. Surely such scents are as beautiful as incense wafted before the Lord."

"Don't be blasphemous, Abigail." Mrs. Fraser raised a lace-edged handkerchief to her nose. "All this aggravates my summer catarrh. I'm sure it can't be good for you to be mucking about in the dirt all day. It certainly does your complexion no favors."

"I hardly think that matters. I no longer have anyone to impress." Abigail attacked the root of a weed, driving her trowel deep into the soil and extracting it with a tiny grunt of triumph.

"Dr. de Sequeyra agreed that fresh air and exercise would be beneficial." Merry would not see Abigail driven indoors before she was good and ready.

Head bowed over her work, Abigail's gaze slid toward Merry, and she gave her a wink.

Isaiah approached. " 'Scuse me, miss, you have a visitor."

Mrs. Fraser brushed a stray blade of grass from her skirt. "Inform them I will be there in a moment."

"Not you, missus. The guest is for Miss Lattimore."

"Well." Catherine reclined in her seat and took another pinch of snuff from an enameled box.

Abigail settled back on her haunches. "I wonder if it is Mr. Sinclair? I think he is quite taken with you, Merry."

Merry shook her head. "That is unlikely."

"Catherine, I could use a respite. Why don't we have tea and biscuits in the shade over there?"

Merry hurried inside, brushing dirt from the knees of her gown. Graham Sinclair had seen her looking far worse, but an odd reluctance rose within her to allow it to happen again.

She pounded up the stairs to her spacious guest room and with Hattie's help slipped into a clean day dress. Within a few moments she was respectably attired and progressing sedately down the front stairs.

Sarah whirled at her entrance. "You have landed in clover, haven't you?"

A flicker of disappointment skittered through Merry at Graham's absence. But then she smiled. "For the time being." Sarah's presence meant she must have learned something of import.

"Well, come here and let me tell you what I've uncovered."

They settled on a settee and Sarah bent close. "Last night the first mate of the *Nyriad* came a-visiting."

Eyes wide, Merry waited.

"It seems he was aboard a different ship, the *Phoenix*, a year or so ago. They were just a few miles from port when Mr. Fraser comes out to meet the boat in his cutter. He tells them there is plague in the town, and they should put in at a little island along the coast until the all clear is given. He goes ahead and pays the sailors their wages and gives them their liberty while the ship lies to the lee of the island. Three days later a bit of a squall came up. There were only two or three men aboard the ship, and when the weather cleared, the *Phoenix* had disappeared. Mr. Fraser and the captain, one Asa McKelvy, claimed to have seen her sink."

Merry latched onto the odd phrasing. "Claimed?"

"Yes, it seems no trace of her was ever found, except a few barrels of salt pork from the hold and part of the masthead."

"Were any hands lost?"

"No. The men who stayed to guard her all swore she sank, but my first mate said that none of them ever worked a deck again, but set themselves up in trade."

Merry's brow furrowed. "He believes the ship did not actually sink then?"

"It is his idea that the ship's goods were unloaded, and then she was taken out just ahead of the storm and scuttled."

Merry tapped her lip. "It seems far-fetched."

Sarah's face fell like a child denied a treat.

"But it is something, when before I had nothing at all. I wonder what Mr. Fraser would do if I asked him about it?"

"Oh Merry, don't." Sarah put an urgent hand on her arm. "I have asked about him in the town. He has a reputation as a harsh taskmaster. Rigid as a pike and twice as sharp. It could be dangerous to cross him. Especially if you think him capable of murder."

"Something needs to be done."

"Leave well enough alone. He would swat you like a fly if you get in his way." Terror widened Sarah's eyes.

Merry cocked her head. "You are truly frightened of him, aren't you?"

"Indeed I am, and you would be, too, if you knew what was good for you."

With a swish of skirts, Merry stood. "Come with me. I'd like to introduce you to someone."

Graham's eyes blinked open involuntarily at the click of the door, and immediately clamped shut again.

"Excuse me, Mr. Sinclair. You have visitors." The houseboy sounded far too energetic.

Suppressing a groan, Graham risked opening a single eye. "Who is it?"

"Sorry, sir. Mrs. Bartlesby admitted the ladies and sent me to fetch you. I didn't hear their names."

"What time is it?"

"Nearly noon, sir."

Graham inhaled a fortifying breath. "All right. I shall be down shortly." With a great deal of effort he relinquished his hold on his pillow and sat up. In the next bed, Connor rolled over to face the wall.

A yawn wrenched Graham's jaws apart, and he stood. He reached for his breeches and administered a sharp kick to Connor's bed. Connor continued to feign sleep, but Graham knew better.

"I sense that I shall need your assistance with this interview."

Connor stiffened then flopped over. "You are a cruel, cruel man."

"Stop your grousing and get dressed. There are ladies waiting."

They emerged a few moments later. Graham's cravat was pitifully mauled and his shaving had been haphazard, but at least he could claim the virtue of speed.

He thrust through the parlor door and sketched a brief bow. Merry Lattimore sat on the settee. Her color was high, and her hands fidgeted in her lap. Golden light flared in her dark eyes when she looked at him, and all of a sudden his stock felt too tight. He ran a finger under it to loosen its stranglehold.

"Pardon me, ladies. I was not expecting such charming guests." He crossed to Merry, made his honors, and took her hand.

Merry smiled politely and withdrew her hand. "Sarah, may I introduce Mr. Graham Sinclair. Mr. Sinclair, Miss Proctor is a dear friend of mine and has some information that may well be key to the answer we seek."

Graham turned to the other woman. She was a pretty piece, but compared to Merry a bit flashy. Her hair was piled atop her head and powdered as fashion dictated. Her gown was also rigidly à la mode. But unless he missed his guess, she had not been born a gentlewoman.

Nevertheless, he bowed over her hand. "Miss Proctor. I am most interested to hear what you have to impart."

Connor clomped into the room. It was Graham's turn to perform introductions.

For a moment it seemed Connor blushed as he bowed over Miss Proctor's hand. No. Graham doubted his stalwart companion had ever blushed in his thirty-odd years on the earth. It didn't bear thinking of.

Merry looked as fidgety as a child forced to sit through a Sunday sermon. She might burst if they did not get to the matter at hand.

Miss Proctor soon confirmed his guess as to her background as she recounted the tale she had heard from the first mate. It all fit quite nicely with what Connor had uncovered. Merry had been uncommonly savvy to enlist the aid of her pretty friend. Come to think on it, she'd been far more successful in her attempts at investigation than he would ever have credited.

Graham sat back, forming a pyramid of his fingers. He nodded for Connor to describe what he had learned.

At the end of Connor's recitation, Merry jumped to her feet and began pacing the room, forcing him and Connor to stand as well. "This is it. He has committed murder to cover his fraud."

Graham shook his head. "We must have proof. To accuse a man without evidence opens us to charges of libel and will do nothing for Jerusha."

"They have no more than this sort of innuendo by which to hold Jerusha. Surely everything we have learned leads to him?"

"Even granting that he is guilty of fraud, there is not necessarily a connection to this murder. We have no proof that

Mr. Benning was aware of his machinations. For all that, he may have been a party to the fraud."

The pulse in Merry's neck stood out in stark relief, and her mouth was ringed with a white line. "What must we do?" Her words held the same tightly controlled quality that laced a man's voice in the instant before he issued a challenge.

"We must establish not only why he might have done it, but that he had the means and the opportunity to commit the crime. And then we must find proof that he did so. I am afraid that without proof, there is very little chance of seeing Jerusha freed."

Merry marched home. Truly, Graham Sinclair was the most insufferable man on earth. Why was it they needed no real proof to convict someone, but they must have rock-solid evidence to free them? And he wouldn't even try. Well Merry would find proof, and if she had to, she would shove it down the magistrate's throat.

She thrust open the door to the Benning mansion herself rather than wait on a slave to perform the office for her. She had marched home without pause. Panting, she pounded up to her room and sank into a chair. She dropped her head in her hands.

Unbidden tears stung her eyes. How was she to prove Jerusha innocent? She hadn't even been able to accomplish that feat for herself. If only Father were still alive, none of this would ever have happened. She would be safely home in England, blessedly oblivious to all the ugliness the world could hold.

She closed her eyes tight, trying to check the tears. If she gave way just once she might never stop crying again. She gasped for breath. Her throat burned with the need to scream invectives and hurl blame. She slid to her knees; her forehead brushed the floor. Harsh keening broke from her lips.

Why?

Why?

Why had God done this?

Where had she failed?

The temptation to pray tugged at her.

She had dreamed of vindication. Thought that the restoration of her reputation would restore everything else in her life to its proper place, but it wasn't to be. Her spirit had a hollow space within that she could not fill, and it seemed to be growing larger.

She needed to forgive Graham. He had done everything in his power to correct his mistake. But what if he left again? If she released the last of her resentment, what would she use to guard her heart?

She tried to stifle her sobs. She did not want to be heard. To be found. To have to explain her despair.

Lord, where are You?

At last the great racking spasms passed, and she lay upon the floor, spent.

A cool breeze drifted through the window and caressed her flushed, damp cheeks.

Jerusha would have been accused of murder even if Merry had never arrived on these shores. Mayhap Merry could find purpose in that. True, she had been unable to save herself, but didn't that give her more reason to see that someone else did not suffer a similar fate?

Jerusha needed her. It was time to get to work. She sat up and dampened a handkerchief with water from the guglet on her dresser. She washed her face and rubbed lavender oil into her temples to becalm the headache her sobs had created.

Her face was still red and puffy, but the house was in mourning. It should scarcely be called into question. As she looked at herself in the glass she nearly fell to weeping again. A chasm was growing within her, pulling at her. Her very person seemed held together by nothing more substantial than the lacings of her stays. Her hands clenched around the wooden lip of the dressing table.

She could fall apart after she saw Jerusha freed. But first, justice.

"Master Benning." Graham raised his arm to hail the young man. It had taken long enough to pick the lad out from his identically robed comrades.

Raleigh turned, and a smile ghosted across his features. He took leave of his companions and turned aside to where Graham stood.

"Mr. Sinclair, I had not looked for the pleasure of your company today."

"Would you have a few moments to speak?"

"Certainly, I do not have to attend Mr. Wythe for another hour."

"It pertains to your father's murder."

Raleigh nodded. "I thought it might."

Graham led the way from the campus to a nearby tavern. "Perhaps you'd care for a bite. It's near the lunch hour."

Raleigh accepted, and they were soon seated at a table.

"Can you tell me anything of your father's last night? I understand you met with him quite late."

The boy reddened and stared into the contents of his mug. When he at last looked up tears brimmed in his eyes. "My father and I had a falling out. We were both upset when I left."

"May I ask what caused the rift?" Graham kept his voice low. No use allowing the boy's business to become public.

"He wanted to send me to school in England. He felt that my friends are advocating measures against the crown that come perilously close to treason."

"You did not agree."

"How can it be treason simply to desire a voice in the Parliament that governs and taxes us? Are we lesser Englishmen simply because we are removed by an ocean from our fellows? His Majesty and Lord North have nothing to fear if they but treat us fairly." Raleigh was becoming more voluble. His eyes glinted with fervor, and for the first time Graham began to understand what motivated the radicals.

"What happened next?"

"I left. He asked me to. He wouldn't listen to sense, and I was too angry."

"Did you see anyone about when you left?"

"Not a soul."

"Did he eat or drink anything while you were together?" Raleigh pursed his lips in thought. "Not that I recall."

"Did he mention feeling ill?"

Raleigh shook his head. "He seemed his usual self."

Graham sought for some straw of useful information. "Perhaps he mentioned problems he was having with someone else?"

Raleigh snorted indelicately. "He was too focused on the problems he was having with me."

Graham nodded in commiseration. "I had the opposite problem. My father refused to allow me to enter the Middle Temple and train for a barrister. He and my mother wanted to send me into the church."

For the first time Raleigh put down his mug and met Graham's eye. "Why the law?"

Graham considered. "I suppose that I felt about the law much as you do."

"Me?"

"Of course, you were just speaking of governments and liberty. Laws can restrict freedom or grant it. Can empower the common man and check a king. Can be wielded for good or evil. It only requires men of passion and honor to pursue justice."

Raleigh leaned forward. "I never considered it in such a fashion."

The clock on the mantel pinged the hour, and the boy started.

"I had no idea it was so late. Please excuse me. I must hurry." He stood and trotted away only to return an instant later, half-breathless. "I've just remembered. As I was leaving, Father muttered something about having to have another unpleasant conversation with Mr. Fraser. Does that help?"

Graham's eyebrows rose. "It might. It just might at that."

Chapter 10

Merry tracked down Mr. Porter to his small office. Mr. Benning's clerk scrambled to his feet at her entrance, offering her the seat he had occupied while his underlings disappeared so quickly they might never have been there at all.

"You all right, miss?"

Merry closed her eyes briefly, and then opened them again, allowing the tears to resurface. "I'm greatly distressed about Jerusha."

Mr. Porter turned away, rummaging with a teapot and clay mug. "I've got some tea."

"I don't think she is guilty."

His hands paused in their deft movement. He half turned his head toward her. "I can't say as I agree with you. Though it's sure sad." His words were low and rough as if they cost him something to say. "Truth be told, it don't matter a great deal what either of us thinks."

"Perhaps not, but what really happened matters a great

deal. As does catching the real killer. I need you to tell me all you can of Mr. Fraser."

He shook his head. "That won't help."

"You cannot know that." She raised her gaze to him in earnest supplication. "Please."

"Naw, miss. I think you'd best just leave this sort of thing to the officials. You don't need to trouble yourself."

Merry's patience had nearly run its course. If she could, she would have snatched the knowledge from his head by force. Instead she forced a sweet simper. "I hope you understand that I am here at the direct request of Mrs. Benning. She is most unsettled in her mind about all that has happened and will be evaluating all of the employees most carefully, now that the responsibility for the estate has fallen on her shoulders."

He sank back into his seat across from her, looking as resentful as if he had been bested in a prizefight. "What do you want to know?"

"Had there been a break between Mr. Fraser and Mr. Benning?"

"How did you know 'bout that?"

The answer was there, just beyond her grasp. "What happened?"

"I don't know for sure. Mr. Benning was troubled 'bout something and wrote to ask Mr. Fraser to come right away. They don't usually come till later in the year when the House of Burgesses meets."

"Then the matter was urgent."

"Must've been. Mr. Benning took whatever it was hard. He even started taking a draught to help him sleep at night. That's what poisoned him, you know. That draught Jerusha took him."

"That is what the sheriff believes." She could not allow herself to be diverted into an argument. "Would you say this all happened suddenly? It wasn't frustration that had been building?"

"Sudden as a kick in the pants, I'd say. Mr. Benning was fine; then he read his post and was in a tearing hurry. He tore up his study looking for some report or other about a ship. Took me near a week to get everything filed away again."

"What ship? Do you remember the name?"

His lips pursed, and he looked into the middle distance. "I don't rightly recall. It was *Furnace* or *Feen*..."

Merry's eyes widened. "*Phoenix*."

"If you already know the story, why are you bedeviling me?"

"I'm sorry, Mr. Porter, I don't know the story. It was just that that particular ship has come up before. Did Mr. Benning find what he was looking for?"

"It was right where it was supposed to be. He was just too upset. I pulled it out straightaway when he called me in to help."

"Do you know what it was?"

"A letter of appraisal on the *Phoenix* needing repairs."

That wasn't what she had expected. It certainly didn't seem to be the sort of document worthy of such a frenzied search. She must be missing something.

"What sort of repairs?"

"From what I can recollect, 'bout near everything. There were the usual small things, but they said she needed a new copper bottom. She was hulled once in an action and never did get patched up good. Caused lots of problems. Worse yet, her knees were all but useless, and they'd have had to replace them."

"Is that expensive?"

"It's nearly cheaper to build a whole new ship than do repairs like that."

A glimmer of an idea poked through Merry's confusion. "But she was insured?"

"Oh yes. All the ships and goods are insured. Mr. Benning was no fool."

"Insurance wouldn't pay for routine repairs though. Only if the ship were lost?"

"That's right."

Merry sat back. It explained a great deal. If Fraser received the same report, he may have just grabbed at the chance to make as much profit as he could. By offloading the cargo, he was paid for it several times, once by the private insurance he obtained, once by the joint policy, and once by whomever he had eventually sold it to. And he did not have to pay for any costly repairs for the *Phoenix*. It must have seemed the perfect opportunity.

But then somehow Mr. Benning had figured it all out and summoned him to Williamsburg. Fraser must have known his time was limited.

"Do you have the letter of assessment?"

He shook his head. "Mr. Benning took it somewhere."

"Where?"

"I don't know."

"Would you recognize it if you saw it again?"

"Probably."

"Do you know if Mr. Benning confronted Mr. Fraser?"

"I doubt it. There wasn't much time for one thing. Mr. Benning was a gentleman. He wouldn't have said anything in front of the ladies."

"Did they meet privately that night?"

"I think Mr. Benning meant to meet Mr. Fraser in the morning. He'd have plenty of time to sort out business." He leaned forward, resting his elbows on his knees. "Look here, Miss Lattimore. I don't see what this has to do with anything. Mr. Fraser is wealthy in his own right. Even if he and Mr.

Benning parted ways, he wouldn't be ruined. He could find someone else to partner up with if he wanted."

Merry looked into the clerk's deep-set little eyes. "You are probably right. I have been thinking too hard."

Mr. Porter blew a gust of air out. "I guess it's been a nasty shock for you ladies."

"Yes, well thank you, Mr. Porter. I can see that I have taken up too much of your time. I do apologize." Merry stood and offered a guileless smile.

Merry found Abigail in the parlor listening to Emma practice on the pianoforte. John sat on the floor at her feet playing with his tin soldiers. The moment he spied Merry he tugged her down to join him.

"You be the French."

John led a whinnying, snorting cavalry charge designed to decimate her forces.

"I'm Colonel Washington," he crowed.

Great swathes of her soldiers fell, and even the artillery could not prevail against such dashing horsemanship.

Emma's piece ended and Merry clapped enthusiastically. Flushed with success, the little girl began a new selection. John, his tongue protruding slightly between his teeth, concentrated on forming new battle lines.

Merry turned to Abigail. "Where is Mrs. Fraser this afternoon?"

"I'm afraid she has a headache. She is resting."

"It's good to see the children so full of vitality."

"God has been so gracious to bless me with them. I was so afraid while they were ill. And then Reginald…" The tip of Abigail's nose turned red as did her eyes. She plucked a handkerchief from her sleeve and dabbed at her eyes. "Excuse me."

Merry placed a hand on her arm in silent commiseration.

She had no words that could heal Abigail's grief. Not when she could not even stem the tide of her own sorrow.

She lowered her voice. "Have you or one of the servants come across any papers that Mr. Benning might have hidden somewhere? Particularly anything to do with a ship named the *Phoenix*?"

Abigail cocked her head to one side. "No. I don't think so. Surely the man to ask would be Mr. Porter?"

"I've spoken to him, and these papers are no longer in the office."

"Do you think it has aught to do with his murder?"

"It could. I do not know, and I would not ruin your good opinion of a man without just cause. Are you certain that nothing odd has turned up?"

"When you phrase it that way, something very odd turned up indeed." From the table beside her Abigail plucked a key wrapped tightly in a bit of paper. She held it out to Merry, who unwound the paper to discover that it was a receipt from Lorring's Tavern for the amount of twenty shillings. A note in the upper left hand read,

Nth Rm, Sep Prv Ent.

"Isaiah brought it to me yesterday. He found it in the pocket of Reginald's best waistcoat. I cannot make heads nor tails of it. Lorring's is far from the best tavern in town, nor is it convenient."

Merry's mind worked as busily as a gristmill as it ground through possibilities. Could Lorring have agreed to hold the papers for Mr. Benning? But then he might as easily have requested a friend do the honor for free and with surer certainty of discretion.

"Mr. Benning did not frequent Lorring's then?"

"Almost never."

The receipt by itself could merely have been for an evening's entertainment, except that it did not itemize the fare or
drinks, as would have been mandated by town regulations.
And then of course, why the key?

Merry looked at the slip more closely. Nth Rm, Sep Prv
Ent.

Could it be that *Rm* stood for room? Tavern owners had to
provide lodging at set rates for travelers. Perhaps Mr. Benning had stayed there? But that made no sense either. The cost
was beyond exorbitant, and he had been on his plantation or
at home; he had not stayed at some tavern, nor would he have
in such a small town, where gossip would have been rife.

Merry gnawed at her lower lip and allowed her troops to
be soundly thrashed again by Colonel Washington.

Tavern keepers also rented out meeting rooms. What if
Mr. Benning had obtained one of those for the long term—
a place to keep the documents he wanted to secure? Somewhere away from his own household, where he knew Mr.
Fraser would be staying. Somewhere with no clear relation
to him. Somewhere safe.

What if the receipt referred to the North Room of Lorring's
Tavern? Was it possible that the room had a separate, private
entrance? An entrance granted by the key growing warm in
her clenched fingers?

Graham settled his hat and left the clerk of court's office.
He'd made good headway. The man was certainly knowledge-
able in any event. And not just about the law.

He picked up his pace. Connor would be waiting at Chowning's. He needed a bit of something to eat. A nice veal pie
and a suet pudding. His mouth watered. He could practically
smell it, though it was unlikely he'd find any. These colonials
seemed to eat naught but pork.

His feet flew out from under him as rough hands hauled

him into the shadow of a narrow alley. An arm clenched tight around his neck. A harsh whisper rasped against his ear. "Let the Negress swing, or you'll be sorry."

Graham stomped on the man's instep, eliciting a howl. A sharp backward thrust of his elbow made the attacker gasp. Grabbing the arm around his neck, Graham twisted in a long, fluid motion, freeing himself and spinning the other man until Graham stood behind him and had the attacker pressed face-first against the wall.

A blow to Graham's lower back made him grunt in pain. Another pair of hands took him by the arms and hauled him backward.

The first man recovered and spun to deliver a sharp kick.

Graham threw his head back, striking the man who held him in the face. The grip on his arms loosened, and Graham wrenched free, but a blow to his stomach expelled the air from his lungs in a whoosh.

He staggered and would have fallen except that a steadying hand righted him. The attackers fled.

He glanced up to find Connor at his shoulder.

"Let's go after them."

Connor shook his head. "They'll have already disappeared. If this was London, I could track them anywhere in the city, but I haven't found my depth here yet."

Graham eased himself onto a packing crate, rubbing his stomach. "Not that I'm ungrateful, but what brings you this way? I thought we were to meet at Chowning's."

Connor grinned. "Seems I've come across some information that might be helpful."

"You're acquainted with the sorts of documents Mr. Benning's business required, aren't you, Isaiah?"

"Yes miss."

"Would you recognize one?"

"I can read, miss. And I know Mr. Benning's hand as well as anyone."

"Then I need your help after supper. I believe Mr. Benning hid some documents away from where Mr. Fraser could easily get at them. We must retrieve those papers. If anyone asks, I will say I am performing a commission for his widow in fetching some papers she needs in regards to his estate."

Isaiah nodded.

"Has Mr. Fraser been in Mr. Benning's office?"

"Every day, miss. And he don't want no help. Locks himself in in the morning and don't come out for meals half the time."

"Mr. Benning was a wise man to move those documents away from his home. If Mr. Fraser should emerge from his seclusion, you must keep him occupied if you can. Find some pretext to distract him from the trial tomorrow. I don't want him thinking to look elsewhere for the report on the *Phoenix*."

"Yes miss. I can do that sure enough."

"Good." Merry sighed. "Then I am going to see Jerusha before dinner. I'd like to give her reason to hope."

Chapter 11

Merry barely kept from sneering at the turnkey. She handed over a shilling and forced one foot in front of the other until she was ushered into the miniscule space that passed for an exercise yard. The sound of the key grating in the rusted lock sent a bolt of panic so strong up her spine that she jerked.

Dread gagged her as the gaol house odors seeped into her pores. She raised a scented handkerchief to her nose, trying to block the stench.

If only she could blot out the memories. Her hands shook so that she nearly dropped the handkerchief. She had not bargained for this welling terror, this absolute certainty that she would never be allowed to leave.

She tried to swallow but could not.

Jerusha appeared, and Merry focused on her face. She seemed to be at the end of a long tunnel. Everything spun and shifted, making Merry dizzy, but if she could focus on Jerusha's face, she could stay upright.

"Miss Merry. I'm right glad to see you."

With a supreme effort of will, Merry unlocked her jaws. "Are they treating you well?"

Jerusha shrugged. "As well as can be expected."

Merry took her arm and pulled her nearer the wall, as far as she could get from the gaoler. Turning away from him, she lowered her voice.

"I believe Mr. Fraser is the murderer. I hope to have proof tonight, and then Mr. Sinclair will be able to present it at the trial tomorrow and have you acquitted."

"Don't you go and get in any trouble on my account. I'll be getting out of this prison, one way or the other."

Merry blinked. She leaned even nearer. "Do you understand what I've told you?"

"You think you might be able to catch the real murderer and get them to let me go."

"How can you be so…calm?"

Jerusha patted her arm. "Time in a cell goes slow. Gives a body plenty of space to think on things. I figure it like this. God holds my life. These folks only think they do. Joseph went through slavery and prison, but it made him a better man. If I hadn't been brought to this country, I never would have learned about Jesus, and I wouldn't have my son."

Merry shook her head. How could Jerusha cling to a God who allowed the innocent to be condemned? If He loved justice so much, why didn't He do something to prevent injustice?

A lump wedged solidly in Merry's throat again. It must be the circumstances stirring up painful memories. Just being in this gaol made her want to scratch through the walls with her fingernails.

"Well, I am here to see that you are not convicted for something you did not do."

"And who put you here, child?" A gentle smile played at Jerusha's lips, but her eyes were probing.

Merry's face felt suddenly cool as the blood drained away. The significance of Jerusha's words resonated within her like a church bell.

"You blame Him for it. I thank Him," Jerusha said.

"How can you be so certain?"

"Even the good Lord was accused of something He didn't do, and they murdered Him for it. Should I expect to have an easier time of it? Nope. He never offered me an easy life, just a redeemed one."

Merry sniffed and dabbed at her eyes. She had never been so prone to sentiment. Jerusha drew her into a warm embrace, patting her back and stroking her hair.

The sobs Merry had suppressed all afternoon were suddenly clawing at her again, along with that sensation of being split in two. But now she knew she must make a choice if she were to be free, whole. She clung to Jerusha as tears streamed down her cheeks.

"There, there, child. It's not so bad as all that. He's protected you, hasn't He? Kept you from real hurt. You can see it now when you look back."

The turnkey entered the tiny courtyard. "Here now, none of that. None of that."

Merry pulled back and mopped at her face with her handkerchief. "I came to comfort you, but seem to have done a poor job of it."

A fresh round of tears interrupted her, but these were gentler, the residue of a heavy storm. When she had regained her composure she continued. "I have to forgive, don't I?"

Jerusha nodded. "If you want to be free." She lifted the hem of her skirt to reveal the manacles around her ankles and the bruised, swollen flesh. "These chains hang on to my body, but they can't touch my spirit. So I'd say yep, you gotta forgive, but also trust. Rest in His purpose. God showed Joseph the reason for his suffering years later."

Merry looked down at her wadded handkerchief. For the first time in a great while a light kindled in her soul. The warmth radiated outward, inching away the coldness of prison that had settled around her heart like a dense fog.

"I think I felt as if God owed me something for my years of living as a dutiful Christian. Never have I taken a moment to consider what He might be trying to teach me." She smiled then and offered a tearful little laugh. "It may have aught to do with humility."

"How is my Daniel?" The question sprang from Jerusha as if she could no longer restrain it.

Heavens. Merry had been so focused on her own heartache she hadn't given a thought to Jerusha's. She took hold of her friend's hand. "He is doing well. Understandably concerned for you. I swear to you, that whatever happens I will do my best to see him freed."

Graham crushed a scuttling roach beneath the heel of his boot. "Are you certain this is where she said to come?"

Connor nodded. "She gave me the name. Said most of the clerks end up here when money runs low."

"I suppose we'll not get away without ordering a couple of pints." Graham settled into a grimy booth, pulling his coattails onto his lap.

Connor's sly grin said clearly that he thought Graham too nice by half.

"Just go order for us, will you?"

Connor made his way to the bar, leaving Graham to sit alone in the squalor and take note of the surroundings. In the afternoon sun, the gin house, den of iniquity though it was, looked more jaded and anemic than evil. But there was no doubt as to the moral character of the occupants. Vice flowed as freely as the alcohol.

Connor returned and plunked down two tankards.

Graham was ready. "I noticed that you could scarce take your eyes off Miss Sarah Proctor this morning. Could it be that the untouchable Connor Cray has been brought low by a convict doxy?"

Connor colored the dull red of terra-cotta. "Watch yourself, boy'o. Miss Proctor has a good heart. Why else would she agree to help a beak like you?"

So his shot had struck home. Graham had suspected something was amiss when Connor had returned to their shared apartments actually whistling. Now his infatuation had been confirmed.

Connor took a slug from his cup. "At least Miss Proctor don't hold me responsible for her transportation."

Graham winced as an image of Merry rose unbidden. Even if she wasn't still outright furious with him, she remained aloof.

Time for a change of subject. "Is the fellow expected?"

"They couldn't say for certain. He comes in most nights, but not always."

"Then we shall have to hope for the best." Graham picked up the grubby tankard before him, eyed the contents, and set it aside.

They passed the next hour and a half in desultory chatter as the crowd in the tavern grew.

At last, the man in question wandered in with a few of his cronies. His short, whip-thin frame and deep-set eyes marked him out as the right fellow, as surely as did his ink-stained fingers among this lot of sailors and journeymen.

Graham jerked his chin toward the man, and Connor approached him with alacrity. For such a big fellow he could move with the swiftness of a wolf when he wished.

Hand resting lightly on the back of the man's neck, Connor steered him away from his comrades.

Graham slid his untouched tankard in front of the man. "Have a seat, Mr. Porter."

"Can I help you gentlemen?" The clerk's fingers closed around the cup greedily, but he still managed to sound superior.

Graham reclined in the booth, using his own posture to put the man at ease. "I believe you can."

Porter could restrain himself no longer. He raised the tankard to his lips and drained it off in a long swallow. Graham gestured for Connor to get the man another round.

"I need you to tell me all you can of Mr. Benning's business dealings with Mr. Harland Fraser."

"I know 'bout you. You're defending the slave woman. Not the kind of work what's going to earn you any friends round these parts, I can tell you."

Graham retained his slouch, but allowed an edge to creep into his voice. "I do not care to curry your friendship. I simply require information."

Porter sniffed, but accepted the second tankard Connor shoved in front of him. "Ain't nothing to tell."

"Had there been a falling out between the two?"

"Why can't you people simply accept that the Negress done for him?"

Graham narrowed his eyes. "What do you mean, *you people*? Have other people been asking?"

"Yeah, that Miss Lattimore what weaseled her way into the household. She's a slick one. She was asking about poor Mr. Fraser just this afternoon. Didn't find nothing out though. Had to admit he were an upright gentleman."

Miss Merry was in a fair way to becoming quite the investigator. He needed to talk to her about not trampling the field before him, however.

Graham plucked a couple of sovereigns from his pocket and allowed Porter to see the gleam of gold. He rubbed his thumb over the topmost coin, and Porter licked his lips.

"Think hard. Did Mr. Benning act strangely in any way before his death? Change any of his habits? Anything?"

Porter's gaze followed the coins as Graham placed them deliberately on the table with a definitive clink.

"There was one thing."

"Yes?"

"He rented a meeting room from Lorring's Tavern for a whole month. His nicest one, too, with a private entrance. No one but Mr. Benning was to go in or out."

"How did you learn of this?"

"I um…happened to see him going in one night and asked around a bit."

"He was not simply entertaining a wench?"

"He never stayed in there for long. And nobody else ever came or went. At least not that I knew. I mean, there weren't but the one key."

"Can you think of anything else?"

Porter held up a hand. "Not a blessed thing. He was a very regular gentleman."

Graham slid the coins toward Porter a half inch, and the man scooped them up, grabbed his tankard, and bolted.

What could Benning have been about in that meeting room? And how was Graham going to gain entrance?

Merry's late-night forays through Williamsburg had nearly grown mundane. So much so that when the night watchman's lantern momentarily blinded her, she was able to summon the aggravated hauteur necessary.

" 'Ere now, where you goin'?"

"I hardly think it's any concern of yours where I go."

"It ain't safe for a lady to be out this time of night. There's bad'uns about what would try to take advantage of a pretty piece on the loose." His lantern swayed slightly, and gin fumes wafted her way.

Isaiah stepped closer to her shoulder, entering the circle of light.

The watchman sniffed. "This fella yours?"

"As you can see I am well protected. Now please allow us to pass."

The man shambled aside, and Merry swept past, her heart pounding in her throat.

A wispy fog settled into the streets, as if Williamsburg were self-conscious of its taverns and gin houses and trying to hide them from view.

"Maybe I ought to lead the way, miss." Isaiah spoke in a hushed tone, looking over his shoulder as if expecting to be set upon.

Merry licked her lips. "Yes, I believe you are right."

Within moments they stood before Lorring's Tavern. Isaiah led the way around the back. Merry produced the key and handed it to him. He inserted it in the lock, and it turned smoothly.

Despite her bravado, there was a chance that someone would disbelieve her tale of an errand from the Widow Benning. The threat of being sent to gaol struck her anew, paralyzing her. She inhaled and closed her eyes tight.

She had made her decision. She would have to trust God to see her through the next step, even if she couldn't see the way herself.

Swallowing the acrid taste of dread, she crossed the threshold. Her heartbeat pulsed in her ears as she surveyed the scene. The very ordinariness of the narrow chamber settled her nerves a bit.

A table, a handful of chairs, a sideboard, and a small secretary occupied the room. Even the walls were spartan, containing only a map of the colonies over the fireplace mantel and a few wall sconces decked with half-burned tallow candles.

Isaiah moved toward the lamp on the table.

"No," Merry whispered. "Make certain the curtains are drawn first."

He did as bidden. His tug on the drapery sliced the moon's light from the room.

Merry groped forward. Her toe cracked against the table leg, and she swallowed a howl.

"You all right, miss?"

Her affirmative came out as more of a whimper.

The light flared, and she found him eyeing her with concern.

"Stubbed my toe. I'll be fine." She turned to the secretary and pulled it open.

For several moments the only sound was the rustling of paper. The letter of assessment, whatever had spurred Mr. Benning's summons, it had to be here—somewhere. She refused to believe differently. But the moments sped past. They had to hurry.

Lord, please help us find these things. Grant that justice is done in this matter. The prayer tumbled through her, and with it came a sudden release of the worst of her tension. The responsibility for this endeavor did not lie solely with her. Jerusha had been right. Even if she failed, God's plan would not be thwarted. Even if she never understood the purpose of the suffering, God knew, and in the end His judgment was the only one that would matter.

Fingers no longer trembling, she paged through the last of the documents. They were all as dull as drainage ditches. Nothing.

"Isaiah, perhaps you could search the sideboard."

Gnawing at her lip, she sat back in the seat and surveyed

the narrow wooden desk. With all its cubbyholes and crannies, it reminded her of her father's desk. She bolted upright.

Could it be possible?

Her fingers groped beneath the shelves. Father's desk had had a secret compartment that would open only if one knew the trick. Her fingers brushed the edges of each nook.

"Ouch!"

Isaiah looked up as if wondering how she had possibly managed to injure herself while sitting still. "Miss?"

She pulled her finger from her mouth. "Splinter."

He nodded and turned back to the sideboard.

"It must be here somewhere." She stood and turned. Her eyes measured and noted every inch of the room. This secret office was too coincidental not to play some significant part.

She stopped in her perusal and turned back to the map on the wall. Was it the uncertain flicker of candlelight, or was there a bulge in the map's canvas?

She crossed to it and eased it from the wall. A thin leather folio dropped from behind the map and thunked to the floor.

A scraping sound from outside snapped their heads up as sharply as the wind tugging at laundry on a line. Their gazes met and Isaiah bent to blow out the lamp. He scrambled behind the curtains while Merry snatched up the folio, dropped to the floor, and crawled beneath the table.

She pulled her knees up to her chin, making herself as small as possible. The door swung inward, allowing a tiny slice of moonlight in with it.

Her ears strained to the bursting point, alert to every rustle and scrape. The intruder was quiet, but her sensitive fingertips detected his approach by the give in the floorboards. Her own breathing rasped unnaturally loud in her ears.

He rounded the table, and she realized that there were at least two of them. One on each side of the table. She was trapped.

"The lamp is hot." The whisper sounded taut. "Someone has been here."

How many of them were there? Merry shrank farther in on herself. Maybe she could crawl out the other side and through the door before they noticed her.

No such luck. The lamp leaped back into life, illuminating the chamber. It might as well have been broad daylight.

A chair slid away from the table, and a man sat down, his knee nudging her.

Merry scrabbled for the other side of the table, but a hand had hold of the back of her skirt and dragged her inexorably backward.

The intruder hauled her clear of the table, and she landed on her backside with a thump.

Graham jumped back, rapping his elbow sharply against the table. "Merry!"

"Graham?"

"What in the devil were you doing under there?"

"Hiding. What are you doing here?" She struggled to untwine her feet from her skirts and stand.

He grimaced. "You must know. I'd venture you are here to the same purpose."

She thawed a bit. Her chin lowered and a sheepish smile flirted with the corners of her lips. "I believe we have just discovered the documents we sought."

"We?"

Isaiah stepped from behind the curtains. Just two feet away from where the man had been hiding, Connor sucked in a choked gurgle.

Graham turned back to Merry, and she cast a superior smile in his direction and held up a thin portfolio.

In the wavering lamplight, Graham fumbled with the string holding the documents closed.

"C'mon." Connor flapped a hand, urging haste.

At last he had it. He unfolded the stiff leather and removed several sheets of parchment.

The heads around him bent even closer. Merry pressed against his side, her hair so close he could smell lavender. The desire to slip a hand around her narrow waist and draw her even closer blinded him for a moment.

What was he doing? He yanked his attention back to the matter at hand with brute force. The first document proved to be a letter of assessment for the *Phoenix*, produced by a shipbuilder in Norfolk.

"This is it." The warm whisper of Merry's words caressed the nape of his neck, and he swallowed hard.

He turned to the next page. "What is this?" The penmanship was childish at best, blotched and nearly unrecognizable.

Dear Sir,
  I have knowlige that may be of use to you. There is a more to the sinkin of yor ship then you been told. If you are intrested maybe we can reach turms. I will call at yor convenince.

                              Jim Nash

Behind this was an affidavit drawn up, signed, and even properly notarized.

They all hunched forward to read it.

Merry gasped as she came to the end of it. She looked to Isaiah. "Fraser turned the *Phoenix* into a pirate ship."

Graham rubbed the back of his neck and chuckled. Now this was motive for murder. What a devious mind the man must have to dream up such a scheme.

"Then they didn't scuttle the ship?" Connor said.

"No. He must have used his ill-gotten gain to refit her and put her into service terrifying his competition along the South

Carolina coast." Graham grimaced at the man's audacity. "A nearly perfect plan. If the ship were ever hauled to, he could deny any knowledge. As far as he knew, it had sunk."

Merry picked up the thread of the story. "But this Jim Nash had been a mate on the *Phoenix* and knew her top to bottom. He recognized her and brought the story to Mr. Benning. Surely now we have Fraser."

She turned to face him, and Graham's chest tightened. He couldn't think clearly when he was so near her. He backed away a step. "We are certainly a good deal closer. Connor, we need to find this Jim Nash."

"Yes sir."

"We must determine how Fraser managed to introduce the poison. I have pondered the problem all afternoon and have been unable to discover a satisfactory conclusion."

"It seems doubtful it was introduced during dinner." Merry ticked off one finger. "And I have not discovered that they met afterward." She looked back at Isaiah.

"That's right, miss."

"Nor did they meet before dinner. I spoke to Master Raleigh today, and he said that his father mentioned an unpleasant interview he would be having with Fraser. But he didn't say when."

"That's right, sir," Isaiah said. "They hardly have time to say 'good day' to each other before dinner. Mr. Benning would have waited for a better time to conduct business."

"What does that leave us with?" Graham had to distance himself from Merry's warmth and sweet smell. He took to pacing the narrow confines of the room, a finger raised thoughtfully to his lips. As if he could think of anything but pulling Merry close to him.

Connor pushed himself away from the wall he had been holding up. "When did the Frasers arrive?"

Isaiah rubbed at the stubble on his chin. "The morning before the family got home."

Merry tilted her head. "We took the children out to the plantation for a few days. We were supposed to be home a couple days earlier. But didn't arrive until the same day you did."

Perhaps they'd gotten the wrong end of the stick. If the poison had not been introduced that day... Graham whirled on the old slave. "Did Mr. Fraser have the use of Mr. Benning's study during that time?"

"Yes sir."

"And Mr. Benning was already upset with him?"

"Yes sir."

"One more question. Did Mr. Benning habitually take anything in the evening? A glass of brandy or port?"

Isaiah shook his head. "No sir. I mean, he did sometimes, but not regular-like."

Graham hung his head. Blast. Mr. Benning had been known as a man of regular habits. Surely it was likely that the murderer had counted on that foible to execute his plan. Nothing else made sense.

"There was his tincture though."

"What?"

"A patent medicine Mr. Benning swore by. Said he'd never had a day's sickness since takin' that stuff."

"Had he been taking this medicine long?"

The corner of Isaiah's mouth quirked up. "At least five years. He hid it in his study though, and took it before bed each night 'cause Missus didn't like it. She said it was quackery, and it'd kill 'im one day."

"And it did." Graham smacked his hands on the desk. "Fraser must have known the jig was up and set out from Charles Towne with murder in his heart. Things worked perfectly to his purposes. He was familiar with Benning's habits. All he need do was place the poison in the medicine and then wait for Benning to poison himself."

"If we find the bottle, perhaps an apothecary or chemist can discover if it yet contains poison." Merry's eyes glittered so brightly with hope that it hurt to look at her. What if he should yet fail?

"Surely Fraser will have destroyed it," Connor said.

"We must at least look," Merry said.

Graham held up a hand. "Merry, if you find it, bring it to me before court in the morning. If I do not hear from you, I will assume it was destroyed. Connor will search for this Jim Nash. By the grace of God, we will save an innocent life."

Chapter 12

Merry bounced impatiently from one foot to the next as she waited for Isaiah to produce the tincture.

A grin nearly split her face in two as he pulled a small green bottle from the very back of the desk drawer.

Professor Cardew's Tincture for the Restoration of Health and Spirits.

"We have him." It was only then she looked up to find Isaiah frowning. "What is it?"

"This here's empty. He weren't even halfway through his last one. I knows 'cause I always bought the new ones for him."

Her spirits plummeted like a pheasant hit by a fowling piece. "I had so hoped." Sighing, she pressed the bottle tight. "Perhaps the chemist will be able to swab it out and get enough to test." She tried to smile.

"I'll be praying on it, Miss Merry. You can be sure of that."

"Thank you, Isaiah."

She trudged up the stairs to her room. Thank heavens for Graham. At least he would do all he could for Jerusha. She could not ask for a more valiant defender. Her cheeks warmed at the thought of his head bending nearer as he inhaled the scent of her hair. In decency she ought to have pulled away, but she couldn't. He had seen her at disadvantage so often that she could not refuse the opportunity to be attractive in some measure.

She unpinned her hair and rang for Hattie to help doff her finery.

The memory of his shock at finding her beneath that desk brought a smile to her lips. He had looked fit to faint. How ironic that his breaking in to a tavern had proven to her he was a man of principle, just as her father had always believed.

Lighting a candle required too much effort. Once Hattie had helped her from her bodice and skirts, Merry slipped into her nightdress and headed for bed. Even if she could not fall asleep, it would be nice to stretch out and close her eyes. It was almost over.

The sheets were cool as she slid between them. She rested her head on the feather pillow and allowed her eyes to drift shut.

Her foot nudged something and she froze. A bed warmer gone cold?

Something shifted. Slithered. Searing pain sliced through her foot. She screamed. Flailing against the covers that seemed to pin her in place, she rolled from the bed, landing with a thud on the floorboards. Tears stung her eyes. Her foot throbbed. She couldn't stand. She crawled away.

Her door was flung open, and Daniel rushed in. Hard on his heels, Abigail, the Frasers, and several of the slaves poured through the door in search of the commotion.

Merry pointed with a shaky hand to the bed. "Snake."

Snatching up the tongs from the fire, Daniel prodded the

bedclothes. Abigail joined Merry on the floor, wrapping her in an embrace. "Are you injured?"

Merry held out her foot.

Abigail covered her mouth in horror. "Dear Jesus."

Daniel pulled the writhing snake from the bedding. Its scales glinted in the candlelight, streaks of tan and brown and cream. About a foot and a half long, it twisted this way and that, heaving its body in hopes of escape. Its hiss filled the room as all other sounds died away in the awful horror of watching it.

"It's a copperhead." Daniel's round eyes and fearful somberness hit Merry as if he'd struck her in the stomach. How long did she have? Would the venom kill her quickly and painfully? Or slowly and painfully?

Tears rained down her cheeks. There were so many things she should have done. She ought to have apologized to Graham. She needed to see him one last time, to tell him how much his help had meant to her.

Abigail dabbed at the twin wounds on Merry's foot, but the trickle of blood could not be staunched. The skin around the bite was puffed and swollen already. Where was the poison? Had it found its way to her heart?

The snake continued its frantic gyrations as Daniel backed from the room. With a dry rasp of scales it broke free and landed in a writhing mass on the floor. The onlookers screamed and scattered. Abigail grabbed Merry's hand to help her scoot out of the way.

Isaiah struck it and then struck again with a poker until the creature stopped its movement.

Quiet descended on the room. Merry couldn't stop shaking. She breathed in for what seemed like the first time in several minutes. Abigail removed her own shawl and wrapped it around Merry's shoulders.

At the forefront of the spectators, Mr. Fraser inspected

the snake's carcass. "That's no copperhead. It's only a water snake. A good look-alike, but you can tell by the banding."

"Then it's not poisonous?" his wife asked.

"Not at all. The bite will hurt like the devil, but it won't kill her." He addressed his comment to Abigail, as if Merry weren't in the room.

It didn't matter. Merry drew in a breath and clasped her hands together to still their trembling. It wasn't poisonous. *It wasn't poisonous. Thank You, Lord.*

"But how did it get in here?"

Mr. Fraser scratched at the stubble spotting his jaw. "Could've come in through a window. Probably just looking for a warm place to hole up for the night."

Merry didn't bother forcing away her grimace. Hopefully it would be chalked up to the pain in her foot. The effort of being courteous to this man would choke her. "I shall be checking my sheets after this, you can be sure."

The spectators drifted away, and Abigail gentled Merry into a seat. She washed and bound the wound with clean linen bandages. Daniel produced a cup of hot tea for each of them, and Abigail insisted Merry drink every drop before tucking her back in bed.

At last, Merry was left alone. Unwilling to stretch out fully in the bed, she pulled her knees up to her chest. She tossed and turned, unable to find a comfortable position. Unable to rid her mind's eye of the glistening image of the serpent. At last she stood.

Regarding the bed with distaste she licked her lips. *Dear Lord, help me.* With a jerk at the covers she dislodged them. Determined to prove to herself that nothing else lurked beneath the blankets, she pulled all of the bedding away from the mattress.

She remade the bed, smoothing the sheets into place and tucking the edges beneath the mattress so that nothing else could crawl in. She replaced the quilt as well and, hands on hips, stepped back to admire her handiwork. Soft living hadn't yet robbed her of domestic skill.

Her gaze caught on a scrap of fabric peeking from under the frame of the bed, and she bent to retrieve it. It was a coarse linen sack with a gaping drawstring mouth. Where had it come from? There had been several people in the room earlier. She had not noticed anyone carrying a sack, but mayhap one of them had dropped it. But then why not retrieve it?

What if the snake had been in the bag? If the opening had been left slightly open the creature would have slithered out, leaving the bag to get caught up in the bedclothes. It must have felt threatened and lashed out when she climbed into the bed. But all that required a planner, someone who had found that snake and deliberately placed it in her bed.

Her extremities went cold again, and the trembling returned. Had they known it was essentially harmless, or did that malevolent hand believe it to be a copperhead?

Graham scrubbed at his face with the palm of his hand as he stepped from Mr. Benning's secret office. The poor man had no doubt known in part that he was up against a dangerous adversary. But it seemed he had never anticipated the depths of his partner's selfish malice.

Of course, Fraser probably saw it as a matter of self-preservation. If news of his fraud and piracy became public, his life was forfeit.

With a clap on Graham's shoulder in farewell, Connor departed to make the rounds of the taverns in search of Jim Nash. The idea of bed and a good night's sleep called to Graham. He had a case to organize, however.

He passed from the narrow alley he had taken by way of shortcut to find an eerie glow smudging the sky before him. Anxiety plucked at the pit of his stomach. He picked up his pace. A whiff of smoke scratched his throat, and he hurried faster. Somewhere down the street the night watchman's bell began to ring.

Above his head, shutters were flung open and footsteps pounded.

He was racing now. In his gut he knew even before he rounded the final corner that it was Mrs. Bartlesby's home on fire. He had never considered that he might be bringing trouble down on her head with his quest for justice.

As he neared the house a spray of sparks flared from the roof over the kitchen. Soot and hot ash rained down like the snow of hell. The slaves were salvaging what they could. Others had formed a bucket brigade and worked feverishly to douse the kitchen wing and keep the fire from spreading.

Graham dashed in through the front door and bounded up the stairs. Smoke swirled about him, making his eyes stream and his breath hitch in his throat. In his room he tossed everything that came to hand into his trunk and dragged it out to the safety of the street. He made another trip, forcing himself up the stairs two by two. If this fire had been set because of his presence in the household, the least he could do was save what he could for his landlady.

His eyes watered, and he covered his mouth with his forearm to block the smoke. Another flight and he flung open the window sash. They would never get it all out by the stairs. It was time to find a quicker route.

First to go were the linens and bolsters. Graham flung them through the window and watched as they plummeted to the ground. Hopefully they would make a bit of padding for other things.

He caught the attention of the houseboy and began to toss down more fragile items.

Dark figures whirled and cavorted below in frenzied activity. More windows were opened and household goods flapped and fluttered through the sky. Orange flames glistened off the windows and water doused on the buildings.

Through the swirl of light and haze and the confusion of frantic movement, Graham spied a figure standing perfectly still. The fire flared, illuminating the form of Cleaves, looking like a giant beetle in his round hat and too-shiny coat.

"Surely you don't mean to go to that vulgar trial?"

Merry glanced up from her porridge at Mrs. Fraser. "It had been my intention."

"Why would a lady desire to mingle with the uncouth rabble? I think it most unseemly."

Abigail met Merry's gaze, her eyes pleading. "I should be most grateful if you would stay with me. Catherine has convinced me of the impropriety of attending a criminal trial, unless called upon by the law."

Merry dropped her spoon with a clatter and gritted her teeth. Catherine Fraser had to be the most interfering, pompous woman in all the colonies. Had it not been for Abigail she would have flouted the woman simply for the fun of it. As it was, she inclined her head. "As you wish."

"Thank you, my dear," Abigail said.

Merry stood and pushed away from the table. "Do you mean to work in the garden this morning?"

"That's a wonderful idea. I need to do something that will keep my mind from all that is occurring."

"I shall join you soon." First she had to find Daniel and ask him to convey the patent medicine to Graham along with her hopes that the dregs could be analyzed.

She hastened to her room and quickly changed from her morning gown to something more suitable to gardening. Her fingers fumbled with the pins as she secured a voluminous apron in place.

She reached for the tincture bottle but stopped short. It

wasn't there. Heart pounding in her ears, she tried to convince herself not to panic. Mayhap it had been knocked to the ground during the commotion last night.

She knelt and peered under the wardrobe.

Nothing.

Not even a dust ball.

On hands and knees she twisted to peer under the bed. She investigated every corner of the room. It had to be here somewhere.

But no. It had disappeared.

She sat on the floor and covered her face. Fraser could not have placed the snake in her bed in order to obtain the tincture, but perhaps he had spied it during the confusion and taken the opportunity to snatch it.

She remembered Fraser's oh-so-helpful advice about the snake. He was a master at turning situations to his advantage.

Even if she could find the tincture now, there would be no time to have it tested.

She had failed.

"Step forward, sir, and be admitted to the bar."

Graham did as bidden. He had provided his credentials to the clerk of courts the day before and now all that remained was the ceremony.

He passed through the swinging gate in the half rail and was granted the privilege of arguing cases before the court. He could not resist a glance back at the door. Where was Connor? Had he found Jim Nash?

"I must tell you, Mr. Sinclair. It is most unusual for a slave to be granted benefit of counsel." The plump, official gentleman formed a steeple of his forefingers. His half-moon spectacles and balding pate made him resemble Benjamin Franklin.

"I am certain that is because there are rarely such serious circumstances involved. Most do not require benefit of counsel, but in such a case…" Graham waved a hand as if his argument were self-evident. "There is more than usual reason to be cautious."

"I am not certain I fully appreciate your case. Do you mean to imply some sort of uprising if this Negress is denied counsel?"

Graham had meant to imply just that, but he had the sense to deny it. Playing to one of the greatest fears of a plantation owner had to be done cautiously. "The clerk of courts and I have searched the archives, and there is no charge against it."

"Neither is there precedent or provision for it. I cannot tell you the last time we had a lawyer appear in hustings court."

"Yes sir, I know criminal matters are usually tried in the court of Oyer and Terminer. However, since the accused is a slave, this venue is her only recourse. You gentlemen have the final say as to her sentence."

The semicircle of solemn gentlemen nodded.

"Gentlemen, this is not the usual petty matter you must decide where the complainant is no more schooled in the law than the defendant. Consider the implications. Justice would be made a mockery if the crown is permitted the representation of counsel in the person of the prosecutor, but an unlettered and defenseless slave woman has no one to speak for her. That, gentlemen, is not sound English justice. It is murder by another name."

Had he gone too far? These speeches must be judged to a nicety. His cheeks burned and he longed to loosen his stock. He dabbed at his brow with a handkerchief, and yet when had he last felt so alive? His magistracy had left him jaded. It felt good to be able to throw himself wholeheartedly into a cause.

The chief magistrate seemed to be waiting for Graham's next argument, so he continued. "Consider it in this fashion. Say she was said to have killed not her owner, but another man. Would not her owner have the right to protect his property by obtaining counsel on her behalf? I would think that if you precluded this basic right that the plantation owners of this country might have a word to say. You colonists are notoriously protective of your rights."

The magistrate's bench put their heads together in murmured conversation.

The chief magistrate finally settled back in his seat. "I fear you shall have a difficult time convincing a group of Virginians to acquit. We are likely to err on the side of caution. It would never do to allow slaves to think they can get away with murder. However, I find that if a lawyer is intent on wasting his time, I have no cause to prevent him—no matter how futile his cause. I shall grant your request."

Graham bowed his head. "Thank you, sir."

"Return after the noon hour, and we shall hear out this matter."

Graham half sprinted from the courtroom. Where was Connor? Had he found Nash or not? He peered up and down Duke of Gloucester Street.

Jerusha's son, Daniel, barreled around the corner of Chowning's Tavern, prompting outraged squawks from the men loitering there as they awaited their chance to be heard in the courtroom.

"Whoa there, lad." Graham placed a hand on the panting boy's shoulder. "Did she find the tincture? Do you have it?"

The lad swallowed, trying to find his voice. "Miss Merry—"

Graham nodded. "Yes?"

"She." He gasped again, kneading his side as he tried to find his breath. "She found it."

Triumph shot through Graham, a hot burst of flame that made him want to crow like a rooster.

"This morning…gone."

The thrill was quenched as surely as if someone had dunked him in a rain barrel.

"Tell me all of it."

In short, gasping sentences, Daniel poured out the tale of the snake and subsequent loss of the tincture.

Graham's lips compressed together as if each word were a vise. He had to put an end to Fraser before he attempted to harm Merry again.

A dray cart pulled to a rumbling stop beside him, and Connor heaved himself from the back. With a tip of his hat he called his thanks to the driver, and the cart ground forward again.

"Where have you been all night?"

"Had to go out to Yorktown."

"Well?"

"It's bad news, I'm afraid. Nash is dead. Drowned, a week ago."

Graham could hear nothing above the buzzing in his ears. Fraser was going to get away with murder and an innocent woman was going to hang.

Connor's brow bunched. "What else has gone wrong? And don't bother to deny it. Your eyes are as bloodshot as an old hound."

"Our lodgings nearly burned to the ground last night. Merry was bitten by a snake in her bed, and the tincture has been taken."

For once he had managed to astonish his laconic friend. Too bad he could derive no enjoyment from this particular situation.

Beside Graham, Daniel stiffened and went tearing across the street. Graham reached to snatch him back, but missed.

"Mama!"

Pressed between two turnkeys, hands manacled in front of her, Jerusha appeared haggard. As they neared the courthouse, colonists clumped around her, both men and women, jeering and taunting. A rock hurtled through the air striking her cheek only an inch or so below her right eye. Blood spurted, and she staggered between the guards.

Graham elbowed his way through the mob until he stood in front of her. She was on her knees now. Garbage and rotten vegetation pelted her. Daniel clung to her, trying to shield her with his body. Graham held up his hands.

"This is unworthy!"

At the sight of his well-dressed form and authoritative manner, the crowd quieted somewhat.

"I say, this is unworthy. I had heard that Virginia is a colony that values justice and the rule of law. How is it that the poorest and most wretched among you can be denied it at the very steps of the courthouse?"

"Murderess." The shout came from somewhere at the back of the mob and renewed the rumbling.

"That is not for you to decide. It may be true, or may not. But her fate will be determined by the King's justice. It is the envy of the world. Why would you seek to circumvent it? Walk worthy of your heritage."

Daniel and Connor helped Jerusha to her feet.

Graham glanced back to ascertain her condition. Blood streamed from the gash on her cheek. It blotched and spotted her pinafore and dress, a gruesome badge of her station in life. His nostrils flared, and his jaw went rigid.

Connor stood at his back, protecting him from assault on that side. God bless the man.

Graham turned back to the mobs, and with his gaze, dared them to make another move. Invariably, the eyes he met turned downward, and the person shifted. With awful slowness the crowd dispersed. When the last of the men had turned tail, he swiveled on his heel.

"Get her into the courthouse quickly." Graham pressed his handkerchief into her hand.

She lifted it to her cheek. "Thank you, sir."

"I'll see you free yet."

Her gaze lifted to meet his, for perhaps the first time in their acquaintance. "I know you'll try. You're a good man." And then she was gone, swept away like street refuse by the turnkeys. Daniel trailed in their wake, his cheeks streaked with tears.

Breathing in through his nose, Graham tried to recover his equilibrium. His fingers ached with the need to pummel something. But Jerusha did not need his skills as a fighter, she needed his skills as a lawyer. Fraser would not win. There had to be a way.

"You did not accept all that bilge about it being unseemly did you?" Merry's spade bit into the earth with extra force.

Abigail looked sheepish. "No, indeed. I would have gone, but…the truth is, I could not bear the thought of seeing Jerusha in such circumstances. Even if she is guilty, I…I just could not."

"Surely you have not come to believe she is guilty?"

Abigail dropped her trowel in her lap and sat back on her heels. "Oh Merry, I don't know what to believe. My mind keeps coming back to the thought that if it is not Jerusha, it was someone else I know and care for. She was terribly upset at the thought of Daniel being sold. She was certain he'd be put to work in the tobacco fields or the rice paddies and die within the year, even though I assured her that he would be sold as a houseboy."

Catherine Fraser strolled near and waited as her slave woman set out a little folding bench. With a graceful sweep of brocade skirts she took her place, holding her parasol so that it shielded her face from the sun. Her handmaid stepped back two paces, near enough to be at hand, not so near that she intruded on the conversation.

"I do declare, all you ladies think of is this garden," Catherine said.

Merry hacked at a stubborn weed. "It is not all we think of. We've just been discussing the trial. We don't believe Jerusha is guilty."

Catherine Fraser's smile died away, leaving her looking as if she had smelled something noxious. "Of course she did it. Don't be silly."

Struggling to keep her dislike from showing, Merry strove for a civil tone. "I lost all tendency for silliness when I was accused of a crime I did not commit and torn from my home."

"I'm afraid her race is prone to lying and sneaking about in order to get their own way."

Merry met the woman's gaze. "I have found every race prone to that particular failing. Even men who by most standards have more than they could ever need have been prodded into crimes by greed."

The barb seemed to strike home. Mrs. Fraser paled and then flushed angry scarlet. "Surely you would not malign a dead man in front of his widow."

"Oh no, not Mr. Benning. I am fully persuaded that he was a most honorable gentleman. Indeed, he was killed precisely because of his virtue."

"Merry…" They both ignored Abigail's tentative voice.

"Then what do you mean to imply?" Catherine exuded haughtiness like a stale perfume. Her manner reminded Merry of Mrs. Paget.

Merry's fingers curled around the spade's handle. Not again. An innocent woman would not be condemned while a pompous, self-righteous prig of a woman could not even be brought to face the truth about her own family.

"Surely you knew that your husband defrauded the insurance company and lined his pockets with the proceeds of turning the *Phoenix* into a pirate ship. He killed Mr. Benning to keep the truth from coming out."

All pretense of amiable complacency disappeared as Catherine tore to her feet. "No." The single word dripped with venom. "It was that slave woman. She placed the poison in Benning's tincture because he meant to sell her mewling brat."

Merry's spine stiffened, and she dropped the spade. She gazed at Catherine Fraser with new eyes. Of course!

Graham listened intently as John Randolph, the attorney general, outlined the crown's case against Jerusha. Despite the fact that the normal course of Randolph's duties saw him practice at the General Court before the governor, no hint of distaste at appearing before the hustings court marred his demeanor.

He kept his message straightforward and easy for the untrained magistrates to grasp, even if he had no proof. According to the prosecution, Jerusha had been in danger of losing her son and had decided to try to end the transaction by committing petty treason, in this case, by poisoning Mr. Benning's evening draught.

Graham would have a great deal more difficulty in holding their attention, much less persuading them to adopt his theory.

"I would like to call Mr. Harlan Fraser to appear before the court." With a courtly gesture, Randolph gestured for the man to step up to the bar.

Graham turned to watch as Fraser took his place. The gentleman duly took his oath and waited politely for the attorney general to commence. His hands rested lightly on the bar. The brass buttons on his bottle green coat gleamed. His tricorn nestled under one arm. His periwig sat squarely in place, but had been so freshly powdered that when he moved it seemed to snow about his shoulders.

"Mr. Fraser, you are a guest at the Benning home, am I correct?"

"Yes sir."

"Indeed, you shared various business interests with Mr. Benning."

"Yes."

"And you were a member of the household when this foul murder occurred."

"Yes sir."

"Thank you, sir. Isn't it also true that on the night in question, you met this Jerusha in the hall?"

"Yes sir. The look she gave me would have flayed a cat."

"Did she act in any way insubordinate?"

"Refused to make her courtesy."

A grumble stirred through the spectators.

"Was she carrying anything at the time?"

"A tray with a pair of glasses on it."

"What time was this?"

"Eight thirty or nine o'clock."

"What did she do with the tray?"

"I could not undertake to say. She carried it into Benning's chamber, and I never saw it again."

"Thank you, sir, for your testimony."

Fraser stepped back from the railing and the attorney general turned to the chief magistrate. "If it please Your Honor, I will now call Dr. de Sequeyra."

With consummate skill, the prosecutor extracted the good doctor's testimony regarding the diagnosis of poisoning.

"Had you any reason to suspect poisoning before your arrival?"

"Oh no. Good heavens, a simple case of acute gastritis I thought. But the symptoms—well, there was really very little doubt you see. They would be recognizable to any competent physician."

The doctor described the symptoms and the steps taken to aid the dying man. "I'm afraid there just wasn't much to be done. Their stillroom maid had already taken steps and administered the correct draughts, but the poison had advanced too far."

"Can you opine as to when the poison had been administered?"

The doctor scratched his nose. "Based on the understanding that the first onset of symptoms was at approximately eleven thirty, I would estimate that the poison had to have been given between eight and ten o'clock."

More rustling and murmuring from the onlookers.

Dr. de Sequeyra might just have lit the tinder that would consume Jerusha.

Chapter 13

"It was you!"

Catherine's lips twisted into a snarl. "What are you gabbling on about?"

"You murdered Mr. Benning."

"Merry!" Abigail scrambled to her feet, and the three formed a taut triangle. "How could you say such a thing?"

"All this energy we have wasted in speculation about your husband's fraudulent dealings, and it was you all along."

Catherine's face burned crimson, but she sniffed. "I think you ought to see the girl to bed, Abigail dear. It is obvious she is suffering from overexposure to the sun. Either that or she is unhinged and ought to be taken to your precious Public Hospital."

Merry's lips curved in a sour smile. "It shan't work, Catherine."

"Really, Abigail, you must do something about your little...protégé. I'd hate to have to bring a libel suit against her."

Abigail stood gaping, her head swinging back and forth to take them both in.

"I finally have the right end. You had as much to lose as your husband. Your dowry is long since gone, and with the extravagant debts you two have acquired it is no wonder he had to set to theft in order to meet the demands upon him."

"Shut your mouth, you venomous little wretch." All trace of good manners and breeding had been stripped away from her demeanor. Her balled fists and belligerent stance were as common as any fishwife's.

"It wasn't about money for you though, was it?" Merry narrowed her eyes, closing the distance between them by one small step at a time. "At least it wasn't the primary concern. For you it was about your status. The grande dame of Charles Towne."

"Be silent!"

"Won't they all be surprised to know your whole life was a facade?"

Catherine's face twisted in torment, and she covered her ears with her hands.

Merry's stomach roiled. But she had to do this. She had to provoke the woman into admitting her crime if there was to be any hope of saving Jerusha. "No more parties, no more credit. They'll all know you are no better than the indentured convicts working in their fields."

"No." A howl of rage surged through the refined woman like a wild creature clawing its way free of a cage. She leaped at Merry, and they toppled together into the freshly turned dirt of the garden.

Merry had tried to force a confession, but she wasn't prepared for the ferocity of the attack. Catherine Fraser was stronger than she appeared.

They grappled on the ground, scratching and tearing at each other.

Abigail stood over them, trying to pull first Catherine and then Merry away. She turned to Catherine's slave woman. "Go get help!"

Nellie looked as if her eyes might pop from her skull. It took her a moment to respond. Merry could spare them little attention. Catherine's fingers had become talons intent on scratching out her eyes.

With every ounce of strength she possessed, Merry held the woman at bay. She brought her knee up between them as Sarah had shown her and heaved Catherine off, flipping her over her head. Merry scrambled to her feet and whirled to face Catherine again, fingers flexed into claws, ready to defend herself.

Panting, Catherine staggered to her feet. Her wig had toppled to the ground, and sparse, mousy brown hair straggled in her face. Her gown was dirtied. Uglier by far was the maniacal gleam in her eye.

"I will kill you, too. By all rights you should already be dead."

"You put the snake in my bed?"

Catherine gave an ugly snort. "That wretched Indian. He assured me it was a copperhead. Can you believe he thought I wanted to eat the creature?"

Her gaze flickered past Merry, settling just over her left shoulder, and something new flitted across her features.

Merry glanced over her shoulder. Several people were hurtling toward them from the house and grounds.

She turned back to confront Catherine with the imminence of her capture and try to reason with her, but the woman had taken to her heels.

Graham straightened his notes. *God help me.*

He stood, allowing the gravitas of silence to descend on

the courtroom and hush the onlookers. It worked more effectively than any request for quiet.

He half turned to Jerusha. "How long have you served Mrs. Benning?"

Her eyes widened and she started. Indeed, it was the first time she had been addressed during the proceedings. "Since she was nine or ten."

"And how old were you?"

"I was thirteen or thereabouts."

"She brought you with her when she married because she did not wish to be parted from you."

"Yes sir."

"Would you characterize Mrs. Benning as a good mistress?"

"Yes sir."

"She was kind to you?"

"Yes sir."

"Did Mrs. Benning get along well with her husband?"

Her gaze cast about the room as if looking for a way to escape answering the question.

The attorney general shot his cuffs. "Your Honor, I fail to see the relevance of this inquiry."

Graham held up a palm. "Sir, if Mrs. Benning is known to have treated this slave woman with great kindness, and she also was on good terms with her husband, does it not stand to reason that she would have exerted her influence on behalf of her servant?"

At the magistrate's nod, he repeated his question. "Did she get along well with Mr. Benning?"

"Yes sir. They were very happy together."

"Do you believe that Mrs. Benning would have advocated for your son?"

"What, sir?"

"Would she have spoken on Daniel's behalf?"

"Oh yes, sir."

The attorney general nearly toppled his chair in his haste. "Your Honor, this is outrageous speculation. Mr. Sinclair invites the Negress to perjure herself with such questions. No witness ought to be so constrained."

"I withdraw the question."

Nodding sharply, Randolph resumed his seat.

Graham walked Jerusha through her activities of that fateful evening. As they had discussed, she answered truthfully, but as shortly as possible.

The crowd in the courtroom was growing restless, shifting from one foot to the other as the testimony continued.

It was time to tread more dangerous territory.

"So in essence, the case that the prosecution has built for Your Honors is based not on fact, but on mere conjecture as to what might have happened. Is this the basis of His Majesty's justice? I say no, a thousand times no."

As his oratorical pace began to accelerate, the crowd once more quieted. He clasped his hands behind his back and paced before the magistrate.

He had only this one opportunity.

Merry lifted her skirts and sprinted after Catherine's fleeing form. For a sedentary gentlewoman, she was as fleet as a deer. Merry's foot shrieked its disapproval of her hurry. The path curved around the corner of the house, and Catherine disappeared from sight.

The tumult of pursuers reached her ears, and Merry glanced over her shoulder. They were not far behind. She charged around the corner in time to see Catherine snatch John up from where he was playing on the lawn and hold him to her.

He wriggled in her grasp, but she tightened her grip until he howled. She bent her head and whispered something in his ear that stilled his protest but set tears flowing down his cheeks.

Dear Lord, what did the woman mean to do? Merry skidded to a halt. John held his little hands out to her. She had to anticipate what Catherine might do. Breathing a prayer, Merry took a single cautious step forward.

She raised a hand as if her fingers could touch John's. She spoke, taking care to sound calm and reasonable. "Catherine, let John go. He's just a little boy."

Catherine backed away a pace. "I don't want to hurt him, but if you make me, I'll snap his neck like a chicken's."

Renewed sobs coursed through the little boy, and Catherine shook him. "Hush."

Merry took another step forward.

"Catherine." Abigail's horrified whisper at Merry's back signaled that the others would be mere seconds away.

Merry stretched out her hand. "It's over, Catherine. There are too many who know."

"Slaves." She spat the word as if it tasted bitter. "They can't testify against me."

"I can." Abigail's firm voice surprised Merry. The woman moved nearer to Catherine, her hands outstretched toward her child. "Let my son go."

"You've always had everything." Hate scored Catherine's words.

"Don't be absurd."

The hue and cry died as the pursuers rounded the corner and witnessed the drama unfolding.

"That's just like you, always so patronizing. *'Don't be absurd',*" Catherine mimicked.

Abigail shook her head. "I mean only that you are blessed. You have wealth, health, and intelligence. What more could you ask?"

"I have nothing." The cry wrenched from her throat was

so ragged it hurt to hear. "But you. You had a husband who doted on you, three healthy children, even the devotion of your staff." Her face crumpled with self-indulgent tears. "My husband will chase anything in a skirt, my five children died stillborn, and my slaves all try to run away. The only thing I have is my standing in the community. Your husband wanted to steal that from me, too."

One eye on Abigail for any sort of signal, Merry continued to edge closer to the distraught woman.

"You're right, Catherine. I ought to have been more compassionate. I have been a thoughtless friend not to see that you have been troubled. Don't punish Johnny for my sins."

Catherine's grip seemed to loosen ever so slightly.

"Mama," John wailed.

Catherine blinked as if waking from a dream. Her grip tightened again as she clutched the boy to her chest. "No! Stop where you are or I will kill him."

Just four or five more paces. As Abigail drew Catherine's attention, Merry inched toward her. Now the woman reeled to her right, brandishing Johnny like an amulet to ward off evil.

"Stay back."

Behind the deranged woman, Merry saw the door to the slaves' hall ease open ever so slightly. She had to draw the woman's attention. "Catherine, you must know that you cannot get away with this. We've caught you."

The door opened a touch more.

"You? You are no better than a doxy. Parading yourself in front of my husband and all society as if you are a lady. It is ridiculous."

Isaiah's head appeared from behind the door and just as quickly disappeared.

Merry eased forward another step. "Not just I. There are too many who have seen your behavior today."

With a guttural cry, Isaiah barreled through the door.

Flinging himself from the stoop he wrapped his arms around Catherine's waist and carried her to the ground. John flew free. Catherine screamed and writhed, scratching and biting.

Merry reached John first. He was bawling, but appeared uninjured. Abigail took him, cradling him close to her chest as she quieted his sobs with the comfort of her presence.

The other slaves piled into the fray, and in a moment they had Catherine Fraser's hands trussed behind her back.

She ranted at the servants, swearing and lashing out with her feet.

Merry hobbled away from the melee. Her injured foot hurt abominably. She leaned against a tree and took the weight off it.

Daniel rounded the house, his eyes going wide and his jaw slack as he took in the scene.

Good Lord. What time was it? Merry straightened and lurched toward Abigail. "We must get her to the courthouse. Jerusha could be condemned at any moment."

"Gentlemen, the widowed Mrs. Benning stands to suffer a doubly grievous harm in this instance. She has already lost her husband, and now she is to be faced with the loss of the services and comfort of her faithful handmaid of many years standing."

Mr. Randolph sniffed.

"Can we bear to allow that to happen on such flimsy evidence as has been presented here? I tell you that I could pick a man from this very room and make a stronger case against him." His palms were damp with sweat, but Graham did not stop his discourse to obtain permission for his little demonstration.

"Mr. Fraser, you were at the Benning house and have testified on behalf of the prosecution. I understand that you were Mr. Benning's business partner and confidant?"

Fraser nodded gravely.

"And yet I could easily suggest that you had access to his bottle of patent medicine, and thus opportunity to place the poison. You had as easy access to lily of the valley as anyone else in this courtroom, and thus the means of committing the crime. To complete a case against you there remains only the reason you might do so." He paused dramatically as if he hadn't thought of that aspect.

A laugh filtered through the small courtroom.

"Yes, that could be a problem." He paused again and then flourished a finger. "But no, I can provide even that. Mr. Benning planned to break off the partnership and expose you because he had discovered you guilty of fraud and in league with pirates."

A collective gasp filled the courtroom, and every head pivoted to peer at Fraser. He seemed rooted to the spot, as if turned into a pillar of salt by the accusation. A scowl deformed his lips as his face turned red and then purple, and at last he sputtered in impotent fury.

"Your Honor." Mr. Randolph sprang up from his bench. "Mr. Sinclair cannot make such accusations without proof. This is the merest calumny. Slander in order to distract this court from his own client."

"Oh, I have proof." Graham held up Jim Nash's affidavit and the letter of assessment. He passed the documents to the clerk of courts.

An expectant hush settled over the crowd as the chief magistrate received the documents. He placed his spectacles on the end of his nose and perused them. After a long moment he turned a speculative gaze on Fraser.

Graham remained as still as if he were confined to the stocks.

The chief magistrate passed first one and then the other document to his colleagues. He lowered his glasses.

"It appears that charges may indeed be forthcoming against Mr. Fraser. However, I do not find that these documents constitute proof of murder."

Avid whispers swirled through the court as spectators nudged and pointed.

"And nor should you, Your Honor. As I said, these documents are proof merely of motive. And yet the case built by the crown against my client is even weaker."

A clamor sounded outside the courtroom, and several heads turned to the noise.

"I am afraid, sir, that we are beyond the stage of looking for further suspects. Have you any proof that this Negress did not commit the crime?"

Graham's heart sank. "Sir, I have further witnesses who were scheduled to appear—"

The courtroom door burst in before a tidal wave of noise. Shouts and curses surged through the courthouse as more people pushed their way into the room.

The sheriff added to the clamor by banging his tipstaff vigorously, but to no avail.

Sitting on the bar, Graham swung his legs over and grabbed Jerusha's arm. He pushed her behind him. Any mob intent on hanging her would have to go through him first.

He caught sight of Merry near the heart of the tumult, and his heart clenched. What on earth?

As fierce as an avenging angel, Abigail Benning strode beside her. She marched straight to the bar. Jerusha's shackles clanked as Abigail thrust little John into her arms. She fixed the chief magistrate with her glare. "Your Honor, I must speak." Her imperious tone sounded nothing like her usual gentle courtesy.

Like the waves on a beach, the crowd receded, and Graham realized that Merry was holding the arm of a bound

Catherine Fraser. They both looked as bedraggled as inmates fresh off a convict ship.

"Widow Benning, I do not deny your right to address us in the matter of your husband's murder, but I do not thank you for this disruption to the court's dignity."

"You have my sincere apologies, Your Honor. However, I believe you will find my actions forgivable. I am come to prevent a serious miscarriage of justice."

The chief magistrate merely raised an eyebrow.

Obviously taking this as permission to continue, Abigail sailed on. "Mrs. Catherine Fraser has admitted to myself and to Miss Merry Lattimore that she murdered my husband."

Graham's jaw fell open, as did the magistrate's.

The crowd surged. Shouts of outrage and peels of laughter mingled with gasps of horror and chagrin.

The only people seemingly unaffected by the pronouncement were Abigail, Merry, and Mrs. Fraser herself. She stared at the wall as if she were alone in the room. Her face grimy and her hair toppled, but not a tear streaked her face.

When his efforts to quell the mob failed to restore order, the chief magistrate gestured to his sheriff. "Clear the courtroom."

When the doors had been shut and barred against the crowd, only the interested parties remained standing before the justices. Fraser stared at his wife as if he had never seen her before.

"You make grave accusations, Mrs. Benning. Indeed, you have opened yourself to a charge of libel if you cannot support these claims."

Abigail outlined the events of the morning. "I still don't know how Miss Lattimore knew to condemn her, but her reactions proved the veracity of the charge."

The magistrate turned to Merry next. "How is it that your suspicions rested on Mrs. Fraser?"

Merry had turned as pale as her fichu, and one hand moved to smooth her hair into place, but she remained composed as she responded. "I had been privy to much of Mr. Sinclair's investigation, and therefore knew that Mr. Fraser had much to answer for in his dealings with Mr. Benning. Indeed, I believed him guilty of the murder.

"This morning, however, whilst working in the garden we were in conversation with Mrs. Fraser, and she mentioned that the poison had been administered in Mr. Benning's patent medicine. It was something Mr. Sinclair had deduced, but everyone else assumed it had been in the draught Jerusha poured. When I confronted her, her actions and words put the lie to her claim of innocence."

The magistrate turned to Abigail again, and the whole story of the afternoon's events came out.

Throughout the proceedings, Mrs. Fraser refused to speak. But she stared at Abigail Benning with a gaze so acid it might have burned a hole through her.

The chief magistrate asked the disheveled woman several questions, which she ignored. She made no movement at all until her husband sidled near and placed his hand on her elbow, urging her to respond to the magistrate. She yanked free of his touch as if he had been an adder.

The magistrate pursed his lips and motioned for his colleagues and the clerk of the court to draw closer. After a brief conference he straightened in his seat and cleared his throat. "It is hereby ordered that Mrs. Fraser be taken to the new Public Hospital for persons of insane and disordered minds."

"No!" Catherine's shriek raised the fine hairs on the back of Graham's neck.

She lunged away from her husband's restraining hands and hurtled toward the door despite the bonds that still secured her hands and arms. With her disheveled hair flying wildly, her face contorted in a grimace, and her eyes frantically darting side to side, she more than looked the part of a madwoman.

The sheriff scrambled from his perch and joined Mr. Fraser in trying to subdue his thrashing wife. The bailiff joined them, and together the three men hauled Mrs. Fraser from the room.

The justices stood, evidently having decided they had heard enough for the day.

Graham wasn't about to let them get away without assigning Jerusha's disposition. He pressed forward. "My Lords, I must ask for your judgment in the matter of this slave woman. Am I to understand that she has been fully acquitted?"

The chief magistrate turned back to him. His eyes held no warmth, but he nodded once. "The Negress is acquitted. Mrs. Benning, take her home and make sure she causes no more mischief."

Chapter 14

Heedless of the disapproving glare of the officials, Merry embraced Jerusha. They had done it. *Thank You, Lord.* An instant later her hands were shaking, and she wished for a place to sit down. They had done it.

If only it hadn't been so awful. Catherine Fraser was clearly unhinged. Still, Merry couldn't help but lay some of the blame at Mr. Fraser's door. His cold greed had led to much of his wife's desperation. Now they were both ruined.

Merry had expected to feel triumph, but she simply felt tired and disheartened.

Abigail turned to Graham. "Mr. Sinclair, I wish you would accompany me to my home. I have a request of you." Abigail held her hand out to Graham, allowing him to raise it to his lips.

There was something different about Abigail. Merry tilted her head, hoping a shift in perspective would reveal the source.

Abigail spoke again. "I fear that I have ignored unpleasantness because I have been too cowardly to face it. It is unseemly. I would most appreciate your assistance in straightening out my husband's affairs."

"Of course, madam."

Abigail nodded graciously and took her son back into her arms. Skirts swinging like a church bell, she turned and swept from the room.

The ride home was silent. The eyes of the townsfolk followed their progress with unwonted speculation. There were none of the heralded congratulations Merry might have expected at the unmasking of a murderer. Mr. Benning's true killer had been apprehended. And yet, looking into the grave gazes of the pedestrians they passed, Merry got the sense that they would have preferred that Jerusha had been found guilty of petty treason and burned at the stake.

Merry ground her teeth. No doubt these good folk resented having their view of things disrupted. For all the recent clamor in the colony about freedom and justice, it seemed no one wanted to extend those things beyond their own social set.

Her heart clenched. Was the entire world the same? If it had not been for her own experiences, she might easily have accepted the status quo. Could it be that God really had brought her to Virginia for a greater purpose, not just to help Jerusha and Daniel, but to fight for justice on a larger scale?

She ruminated on the new thought, and her gaze found Graham's. She owed him an apology. She had known for some time that he was not at fault for her transportation. He had simply been a convenient scapegoat, someone upon whom she could focus her anger.

His gaze continued to hold hers. Could he understand? Would he forgive her manipulation in forcing him to help Jerusha?

* * *

Abigail ushered Graham into the drawing room, and once more was struck with the elegant simplicity of the room.

He took the seat she offered and settled in comfortably.

"Mr. Sinclair, I fear that I have done nothing in the interests of my husband's estate since his murder. I…I had left it all in Mr. Fraser's hands, thinking him trustworthy and capable. Now, of course, there is a different complexion on matters, and I must know if he has managed things as I fear he has. Would you be willing to look into the matter for me?"

"I would be happy to do so, Mrs. Benning. It's wise to be concerned under the circumstances."

"I would also like you to prepare an order of manumission for Jerusha and Daniel."

He raised an eyebrow. "Do you think it will be granted?"

A small smile flickered over her features. "I shall see to it. You may leave that part to me. After what Jerusha has been put through, it is only fair and… Did you see the people in the street? They seemed not at all pleased that the real murderess has been captured. Had Jerusha been alone, they might still have strung her up on some pretext."

"I will certainly do so, but you realize that if she is freed, she will not be allowed to remain in Virginia."

"It will be difficult to let her go, but I will give her enough to get her to Pennsylvania. I have heard that freed slaves can make a life for themselves in that colony."

"It seems you have thought this all through."

"For the first time in a long while I am thinking for myself rather than gliding along the river of someone else's expectation." Her wistful smile was fleeting.

He nodded in sympathy. In some small measure he understood her regrets. He himself had been going through the motions of life for too long. This journey to Virginia, the pursuit of justice, had reminded him of his zeal for the law, and the joy to be found in seeing right prevail.

"There is one more thing I would ask you to consider, Mr. Sinclair."

"Yes?"

For the first time Abigail Benning looked away and seemed at a loss for words. When she turned her gaze back to him it was with an accompanying flush heating her cheeks. "Go to Merry. Confess your feelings for her."

The flush transferred itself to him. He tugged at his already straight waistcoat. "I…I do not. That is to say—"

She held up a peremptory hand. "Please, I would not ask you to expose your affection if I did not believe it might be returned. She is a lovely girl, and you might make each other very happy. If all of this has taught me anything, it is not to squander the opportunities we are given to love and be loved."

He could not move. The air in his lungs seemed suddenly insufficient.

"You will at least consider it?"

With an effort he forced a nod, and she smiled. "Ah, here is Hattie with refreshment. Would you care for tea, or perhaps you would prefer coffee?"

The children's squeals of laughter filled the air as they dashed about the lawn playing tag.

Merry smiled where she sat in the shade of the oaks. There was something infectious about their radiant joy. Beside her, Abigail continued an anecdote about Mr. Benning. Her grief at his death remained, but it was less raw. She seemed to draw a great deal of comfort from the happy memories they had shared.

A figure appeared around the corner of the house and sauntered toward them. Shading her eyes, Merry leaned forward. Her heart fluttered. It was Graham Sinclair. She had tried to find the chance to make amends, but though he had been by the house often in the last few weeks, they had never been alone.

Today she would grasp the opportunity. He would not leave until she had a chance to speak to him.

He neared and swept off his hat. "Good afternoon, ladies." His queue gleamed dark chestnut in the sun. His smile as catching as the children's.

"Mr. Sinclair—"

"Miss Lattimore—"

Trust her to blurt something out just as he was trying to speak. "I'm sorry. What did you wish to say?"

"What I have to say can wait." He seemed relieved.

Merry licked her lips. "Are you certain? I would not mind waiting." She turned to ask Abigail to excuse them for a moment, but she had disappeared. In for a penny, in for a pound. Merry sighed and waved toward Abigail's seat. "Won't you be seated?"

He complied.

"Mr. Sinclair, I..." Tears pricked her eyes. "I owe you an apology. Since my trial I have treated you terribly. I blamed you for all my wretchedness. And I was most unkind. I beg your forgiveness."

He shook his head and seemed about to speak, but she held up a hand.

"No, please. I was innocent, but matters certainly did not give credence to that fact. I shouldn't have held that against you. Particularly when you were so gallant as to secure my pardon and come all the way to the colonies to deliver it to me." She bit her lip. On with it. Confession would do her good. "And then I manipulated you into handling Jerusha's case, though I knew you must wish to return to your own life in England. I've acted wretchedly. I am so sorry."

"My dear girl. Your apology isn't necessary, but since

you've made it, I accept it in the same spirit it was offered. If I'd been more discerning when you first appeared in my court, none of this would have happened."

Her gaze met his again. He had the kindest face. "My father was right to promote your passion for justice. I ought not to have said he wasn't."

"But you were right, too. I had forgotten myself. I was so bogged down by the cases I heard in my court that I gradually forgot that in every instance there were people's lives and livelihoods at stake. I don't know if I would ever have awakened to that realization but for you. Shall we consider it even?"

She smiled. He could be so adept at putting her at ease.

He stood and offered his arm. "Would you care to walk?"

Little bubbles of warmth effervesced through her. He helped her to her feet, and they walked toward the orchard. Fall had kissed the leaves, turning them every shade of red and orange and gold.

"I must apologize as well," Graham said. "In my attempts to find you, I spoke to your mother. She admitted that when she sent me away all those years ago, it had been without your consent. I allowed resentment—"

"What?" She stopped and tugged her hand free.

He looked bewildered. His mouth opened and then shut twice.

She closed her eyes and tears prickled the lids. "She sent you away?"

He nodded. "I thought you knew?"

She shook her head. Despite her effort at restraint, the tears spilled over. She covered her face with her hands. He hadn't abandoned her, he'd been sent away. All this time he'd been as hurt as she. The last few bands of iron that had constricted her heart tumbled free. "I thought you no longer cared."

He drew near, wrapping her in the warmth of his embrace.

"I'm sorry. I'm so sorry," he murmured, his chin pressing gently against the top of her head.

At last she regained her composure. "I ought to have known. She was so determined to see me married off to that odious man."

"No, I should have spoken to you before just disappearing."

At last she stepped away, breaking the embrace. Arm in arm they strolled through the orchard. Their individual sides of the story tumbled out, leaving Merry shaking her head in wonder. Somehow God had orchestrated matters to see them reunited, their pain mended.

The sun flared as it touched the rim of the horizon.

Graham started as if waking from a dream. "I forgot why I've come." He smiled so warmly that something fluttered in her belly. "There is a ship in port. It will head for England before the month is out."

The sun must have plummeted from the sky. The world seemed immediately colder and darker. She tried to keep the regret from her voice. "You are leaving then?"

"I don't think so. Not yet at any event. I thought you might wish to return home." He leaned nearer. "To be honest I find myself enjoying the colonial life. There is an abundance of opportunity here for a man with initiative."

"Then you intend to stay?" She could not keep the note of hope from her voice.

"For a while at least. After your experiences, however, I thought that perhaps you might wish to return to England as quickly as possible."

The notion of returning home felt curiously flat. What was there for her? Her mother cared not a whit for her welfare. There was no position waiting. What claim did England truly have on her? "I thought I wished to return to England, but now I find that the prospect holds little charm. I could make a nice life for myself here. Abigail or Sarah might agree to help me start a tearoom."

"Not tea."

She glanced up at him. "Pardon me?"

"Be a mantua maker or a milliner or open a coffeehouse, but do not go into the business of tea at a time like this."

"Why ever not?"

"Have you not heard of Parliament's Tea Act? People throughout the colonies are abstaining from drinking tea because of the duties imposed upon it, and I hardly blame them."

"Coffee then." She smiled at him. "Do I detect a note of sympathy for these colonists?"

He shrugged, but could not quite conceal his smile at having been caught. "I have been talking to young Raleigh. Though I don't agree with everything his Mr. Henry espouses, it appears that the colonists do have basis for their grievances."

"It sounds as if you propose to become one of these colonists yourself."

He stopped, halting their progress, and looked down at her for a long moment. "I suppose I do. Opportunities abound in this new world. Why should I not grasp mine? I could make a difference. I could fight for justice, for a better system of governance in this land."

Merry nodded. His passion conveyed through the pressure of his fingers on her arm and the smoldering heat in his eyes.

"Your case, and Jerusha's, have opened my eyes to much that is wrong with the current system. Why should people not be accorded the dignity of being presumed innocent? Surely it should be the government's duty, with its greater resources, to prove guilt, rather than for the individual to prove innocence. For an unlettered layman to be forced into proving a negative—it seems more than unfair when I consider the evils it has wrought." He sounded almost angry as he ticked off his points.

"You can do it. With such passion driving you, you'll be able to help shape the course of the colony."

His hand moved to caress her cheek. "Then you believe in me—" His voice choked off, and he groaned, drawing her close.

"Merry. Merry," he whispered, burying his face in her hair. "I have not spoken. I feared you could never be brought to bear any affection for me, but now…"

She turned her face up to his. He gently cupped her face in his hands and lowered his lips over hers. She sank into the kiss, a thrill swirling down into her belly. He drew her even closer, and she went willingly, wrapping her arms about him.

When he at last broke away she was breathless, her knees as wobbly as a new foal's.

"Can you… Is it possible that you could have feelings for me?" His voice was raspy, as if he, too, was a bit short of breath.

"I've loved you since I was a girl and you helped me rescue that bird with the broken wing."

He laughed and pulled her close to him again. "You were so worried about that sparrow."

Her head fit perfectly in the hollow of his shoulder. She could stay like that forever. Safe and secure and…loved. Realization swept over her. God had seen that sparrow fall, and He had made provision for it through her. How much more did He love His children? All the time she had wallowed in the certainty that He and Graham had abandoned her, He had been working matters around to this place. She blinked against tears. No longer fettered, her heart seemed to swell in her chest, ready to burst with blessings. "I'm so unworthy."

Graham stepped back slightly to look in her face. "Not you,

my gallant Merry. You are everything I could ever desire in a woman. If anything, it is I who am unworthy."

He cupped her cheek in the palm of his hand. "We can stay mired in our pasts, or we can look to the future."

Merry tipped her lips up for another long kiss. When she pulled away again she was trembling.

Graham took hold of both her hands. "Merry, will you join your future to mine? I think we can make a real difference in this land. Change other futures, too. Will you become my wife?"

Merry's heart stuttered to a halt. Had she heard rightly? Could God truly be pouring out such blessings on her despite her many mistakes? Her gaze sought his, and the tender sincerity she found there warmed her to her toes. "Yes. Oh yes. Together we can do anything."

* * * * *

REQUEST YOUR FREE BOOKS!

2 FREE CHRISTIAN NOVELS
PLUS 2
FREE
MYSTERY GIFTS

HEARTSONG
PRESENTS

YES! Please send me 2 Free Heartsong Presents novels and my 2 FREE mystery gifts (gifts are worth about $10). After receiving them, if I don't wish to receive any more books I can return the shipping statement marked "cancel." If I don't cancel, I will receive 4 brand-new novels every month and be billed just $4.24 per book. That's a savings of 20% off the cover price. It's quite a bargain! Shipping and handling is just 50¢ per book in the U.S.* I understand that accepting the 2 free books and gifts places me under no obligation to buy anything. I can always return a shipment and cancel at any time. Even if I never buy another book, the two free books and gifts are mine to keep forever.

159 HDN FVYK

Name   (PLEASE PRINT)

Address   Apt. #

City   State   Zip

Signature (if under 18, a parent or guardian must sign)

Mail to the Harlequin® Reader Service:
IN U.S.A.: P.O. Box 1867, Buffalo, NY 14240-1867

* Terms and prices subject to change without notice. Prices do not include applicable taxes. Sales tax applicable in N.Y. This offer is limited to one order per household. Not valid for current subscribers to Heartsong Presents books. All orders subject to credit approval. Credit or debit balances in a customer's account(s) may be offset by any other outstanding balance owed by or to the customer. Please allow 4 to 6 weeks for delivery. Offer available while quantities last. Offer valid only in the U.S.

HSPDIR13

REQUEST YOUR FREE BOOKS!

2 FREE INSPIRATIONAL NOVELS
PLUS 2
FREE
MYSTERY GIFTS

Love Inspired®

YES! Please send me 2 FREE Love Inspired® novels and my 2 FREE mystery gifts (gifts are worth about $10). After receiving them, if I don't wish to receive any more books, I can return the shipping statement marked "cancel." If I don't cancel, I will receive 6 brand-new novels every month and be billed just $4.49 per book in the U.S. or $4.99 per book in Canada. That's a savings of at least 22% off the cover price. It's quite a bargain! Shipping and handling is just 50¢ per book in the U.S. and 75¢ per book in Canada.* I understand that accepting the 2 free books and gifts places me under no obligation to buy anything. I can always return a shipment and cancel at any time. Even if I never buy another book, the two free books and gifts are mine to keep forever.   105/305 IDN FVYV

Name	(PLEASE PRINT)	
Address		Apt. #
City	State/Prov.	Zip/Postal Code

Signature (if under 18, a parent or guardian must sign)

Mail to the **Harlequin® Reader Service:**
IN U.S.A.: P.O. Box 1867, Buffalo, NY 14240-1867
IN CANADA: P.O. Box 609, Fort Erie, Ontario L2A 5X3

**Are you a subscriber to Love Inspired books
and want to receive the larger-print edition?**
Call 1-800-873-8635 or visit www.ReaderService.com.

LIDIR13

ReaderService.com

Manage your account online!

- Review your order history
- Manage your payments
- Update your address

> *We've designed
> the Harlequin® Reader Service
> website just for you.*

Enjoy all the features!

- Reader excerpts from any series
- Respond to mailings and special monthly offers
- Discover new series available to you
- Browse the Bonus Bucks catalog
- Share your feedback

Visit us at:

ReaderService.com

HEARTSONG
PRESENTS

Look out for 4 new
Heartsong Presents books next month!

**Every month 4 inspiring faith-filled
romances will be available in stores.**

These contemporary and historical Christian
romances emphasize God's role in every
relationship and reinforce the importance of
faith, hope and love.

To Trust or Not to Trust a Cowboy?

Former Dallas detective Jackson Stroud was set on moving
to a new town for his dream job, until he makes a pit stop
and discovers on the doorstep of a café an abandoned
newborn and Shelby Grace, a waitress looking for a fresh
start. He decides to help Shelby find the baby's mother,
and through their quest he believes he's finally found a
place to belong, while Shelby's convinced he will move on
eventually. What will it take to convince Shelby that this is
one cowboy she can count on?

Bundle of Joy

by

Annie Jones

Available March 2013!

www.LoveInspiredBooks.com

LI87801